LEGWORK

The man's teeth flashed white and he thrust his blade up and in.

Fargo's boot was already rising. He caught the would-be assassin between the legs and the knife stopped inches from his chest as the man gasped and staggered back, his thighs pinched together from the pain.

Suddenly the woman holding him let go and a knife glinted in her hand.

"I will kill you myself."

She had a slight accent that at the moment Fargo couldn't afford to give much thought. He barely avoided a stab at his throat. Pivoting, he went for his Colt again, only to have the woman do the most incredible thing: she leaped high into the air and kicked him with her right foot, catching him across the jaw. . . .

THE
TRAILSMAN
#340

HANNIBAL
RISING

by
Jon Sharpe

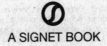

A SIGNET BOOK

SIGNET
Published by New American Library, a division of
Penguin Group (USA) Inc., 375 Hudson Street,
New York, New York 10014, USA
Penguin Group (Canada), 90 Eglinton Avenue East, Suite 700, Toronto,
Ontario M4P 2Y3, Canada (a division of Pearson Penguin Canada Inc.)
Penguin Books Ltd., 80 Strand, London WC2R 0RL, England
Penguin Ireland, 25 St. Stephen's Green, Dublin 2,
Ireland (a division of Penguin Books Ltd.)
Penguin Group (Australia), 250 Camberwell Road, Camberwell, Victoria 3124,
Australia (a division of Pearson Australia Group Pty. Ltd.)
Penguin Books India Pvt. Ltd., 11 Community Centre, Panchsheel Park,
New Delhi - 110 017, India
Penguin Group (NZ), 67 Apollo Drive, Rosedale, North Shore 0632,
New Zealand (a division of Pearson New Zealand Ltd.)
Penguin Books (South Africa) (Pty.) Ltd., 24 Sturdee Avenue,
Rosebank, Johannesburg 2196, South Africa

Penguin Books Ltd., Registered Offices:
80 Strand, London WC2R 0RL, England

First published by Signet, an imprint of New American Library,
a division of Penguin Group (USA) Inc.

First Printing, February 2010
10 9 8 7 6 5 4 3 2 1

The first chapter of this book previously appeared in *Red River Reckoning*, the three
hundred thirty-ninth volume in this series.

Copyright © Penguin Group (USA) Inc., 2010
All rights reserved

 REGISTERED TRADEMARK—MARCA REGISTRADA

Printed in the United States of America

The Trailsman

Beginnings . . . they bend the tree and they mark the man. Skye Fargo was born when he was eighteen. Terror was his midwife, vengeance his first cry. Killing spawned Skye Fargo, ruthless, cold-blooded murder. Out of the acrid smoke of gunpowder still hanging in the air, he rose, cried out a promise never forgotten.

The Trailsman they began to call him all across the West: searcher, scout, hunter, the man who could see where others only looked, his skills for hire but not his soul, the man who lived each day to the fullest, yet trailed each tomorrow. Skye Fargo, the Trailsman, the seeker who could take the wildness of a land and the wanting of a woman and make them his own.

Deep in the Missouri backwoods, 1861—where hate and greed pit brother against brother and sister against sister.

1

There were only two things in life Skye Fargo liked as much as a good card game. One was a willing filly and the other was the warm feeling in his gut from good whiskey. At the moment he was enjoying all three. As the locals in Missouri might say, he was in hog heaven.

Fargo was on the steamboat *Yancy*, a side-wheeler plying its way up the broad Mississippi River toward the small town of Hannibal. He had sat in on a poker game early that afternoon and now it was ten at night and he was on a winning streak that he hoped would continue a good long while. Perched on his lap was a dove called Sweetpea and at his elbow sat a half-empty bottle of the best whiskey the *Yancy* served.

Fargo took another swallow, smacked his lips in satisfaction, and then lightly smacked Sweetpea on her rounded backside. "Stick with me, gal, and this will be a night you won't forget."

"Where have I heard that before?" Sweetpea giggled and fluttered her long eyelashes. She had a full bosom and a slim waist and lips as red and full as ripe strawberries. Her hair was a lustrous burgundy and hung to her shoulders in curls.

Fargo smacked her again, harder. That giggle of hers irritated him. It had a nasal quality, as if she were giggling out her nose instead of her mouth, and made him think of a goose being strangled. She did it a lot. Her voluptuous body more than made up for the annoyance, but if she giggled less he would be happier. And it wasn't as if she was the only irritation. The other was a man named Baxter, a weasel with a needle-thin mustache and a derby who fancied himself a professional gambler and had been needling the other players the whole day. Fargo was growing tired of being needled.

"Are you going to bet or sit there fondling that cow?" Baxter now demanded.

Sweetpea stiffened. "Here now. There's no call for insults."

"Tell that to that slab of muscle you've attached yourself to," the gambler replied. "If everyone put on the same show he does when he goes to bet, poker games would last weeks."

The three other players shifted uneasily in their chairs. They had grown tired of his carping, too.

Fargo sat perfectly still. He was a big man, broad of shoulder, and he packed more hard muscle on his frame than most. It came from the life he led. His buckskins marked him for what he was—a frontiersman. He also wore a white hat nearly brown with dust, a red bandanna around his throat, and boots that had seen a lot of wear. On his hip was a Colt, in a hidden sheath in his boot an Arkansas toothpick. He kept his beard neatly trimmed and had what a lady once described as "the most piercing lake blue eyes this side of creation." Now he raised those eyes to meet the gambler's and the lake blue became glacier cold. "For such a little runt you sure do run off at the mouth."

Now it was Baxter who stiffened. He wore a frock coat that might conceal all sorts of things and during the game had held his left forearm on the table in a way that suggested to Fargo he had something up his sleeve. A hideout, most likely. "I don't like that kind of talk."

"Then you shouldn't go around insulting folks." Fargo added chips to the pot. "I raise you, you little peckerwood."

Baxter grew red in the face. He was short, not much over five feet, and about as wide as a broom handle. "Keep it up."

Fargo gripped Sweetpea by the arm and pulled her off his lap. She frowned but didn't object. Standing, he lowered his hand so it brushed his Colt. "I am tired of your guff. Shut up or show you have sand."

The other players pushed back their chairs.

Baxter glowered. He glanced at Fargo's Colt and shifted slightly so his left arm was pointed at Fargo. "You don't want to rile me."

"I'm plumb scared."

"I mean it. Ask anyone here. I have a reputation."

"Makes two of us."

"Is that so? Just who the hell are you, anyway? I've said my name but I don't recollect you ever saying yours."

"It's Skye Fargo."

The gambler blinked and started to smirk as if he thought it was a jest; then he gave a start and the red in his cheeks drained to a pasty chalk. "I think I've heard of you."

"Could be," Fargo allowed. The damn newspapers were always writing about him.

Another player said, "I sure have. You're the one who killed those outlaws a while back. The ones that robbed that stage. I read where you went up against twenty of them armed with just your bowie and your pistols."

Fargo didn't own a bowie. He wore one revolver, not two. And there had been four cutthroats, not twenty.

Baxter looked sick. He had broken out in a sweat and his fingers were twitching. "You're *that* Fargo?"

Fargo didn't answer.

The other players were staring at the gambler as they would a man about to step up on a gallows. Baxter's throat bobbed and he coughed and said, "I didn't know who you were when I said all those things."

Fargo waited, his hand close to his Colt.

"I saw you look at my sleeve. I suppose you've guessed I have a derringer up it."

Fargo waited.

"If I try to use it you're liable to kill me."

"You'll be dead before it clears your sleeve," Fargo broke his silence.

Baxter started to raise his other arm to his face as if to mop it with his sleeve but thought better of it. "Listen. How about if I say I'm sorry and we get on with the game? No hard feelings?"

"Say it." Fargo had no real hankering to resort to gunplay. But he would be damned if he would take any more insults.

"What? Oh. All right. I apologize. Will that do?"

Fargo slowly sank into his chair. They all heard the breath Baxter let out. The other players slid their chairs to the table and Sweetpea pressed against Fargo's leg and wriggled to show she would like to reclaim his lap. He let her but he shifted slightly so he had quick access to his Colt.

Baxter cleared his throat again. "I never met anyone famous before. Not unless you count a senator."

Fargo refilled his glass and took another swallow. The whiskey tasted flat, and he frowned.

"Mind if I ask what you're doing in this neck of the woods? Folks say you're partial to the prairie country and the mountains."

Fargo's frown deepened. The gambler had gone from being one kind of nuisance to being another. "I am partial to not being pestered."

"Oh. Sorry."

Baxter fell into a sulk. The other players were uneasy and it showed. For Fargo, the joy had gone out of the whiskey and now the game, and he was mad at himself for spoiling things. The next hand, he bet half his winnings on three kings and was beaten by a full house. He could take a hint. He announced he was calling it quits for the night.

Sweetpea stayed glued to his side as he cashed in his chips and watched him put the money in his poke and tuck the poke under his shirt. Beaming, she hooked her arm in his.

"Does this mean we can go for a stroll? I would dearly love some fresh air."

So would Fargo. The cigar and pipe smoke was thick enough to cut with a butter knife.

The hurricane deck was almost empty at that time of night. Over in a corner a couple were cheek to cheek. Another man and woman at the port rail were gazing at the myriad of stars that sparkled in the firmament.

Fargo strolled past them to the jackstaff. Thick coils of smoke belched from the smokestack aft of the deck and were borne away on the breeze. The throb of the steam engine never let up. He gazed down at the murky water and listened to the hiss of the bow as it cleaved the surface.

"I lost a good friend last week on the *Celeste Holmes*," Sweetpea sadly remarked.

Fargo had heard about the disaster. A boiler blew and over sixty people were scalded to death. The *Celeste* limped on, only to run into a snag that ripped her open from bow to stern. According to the few survivors, the boat broke apart down the middle and a second explosion blew most of what was left, and nearly everyone still alive, to bits and pieces.

"They say that pretty near ten boats have gone down in the past couple of years."

Fargo grunted.

Sweetpea bit her lip and twirled a curl with her finger. "I have nightmares about it happening to me."

"If it scares you, why work on one?"

She shrugged. "Jobs are hard to come by. This one is easy and it pays well and I don't have to sleep with a man unless I want to."

Pulling her to him, Fargo cupped her fanny and grinned. "If you want to sleep with me I won't fight you off."

Giggling, Sweetpea pecked him on the chin. "I like you, handsome. You're fun to be with and you treat a girl decent."

"Only until I get her in bed." Fargo nuzzled her neck and was rewarded with a coo of delight.

5

"Why can't all men be as playful as you? Most only want to get the poke over with and be shed of the woman. Why is that?"

Fargo nipped an earlobe and was running the tip of his tongue from her ear to her mouth when the *pat-pat-pat* of rushing feet on the hardwood deck registered.

He reacted in instinct, and whirled.

There were two of them, a man and a woman. Steel glittered, and the man came at him with a knife.

Pushing Sweetpea out of harm's way, Fargo dodged a cut that would have gutted him like a fish. He couldn't see their faces all that well but he was sure he had never run into either of them before, which made their attempt to kill him all the more bewildering. Shaking off his surprise, he swooped his hand to his Colt but before he could clear leather the woman sprang with lightning speed and gripped his arm.

"I have him! Do it!"

The man's teeth flashed white and he thrust his blade up and in.

Fargo's boot was already rising. He caught the would-be assassin between the legs and the knife stopped inches from his chest as the man gasped and staggered back, his thighs pinched together from the pain.

Suddenly the woman holding him let go and a knife glinted in her hand.

"I will kill you myself."

She had a slight accent that, at the moment, Fargo couldn't afford to give much thought. He barely avoided a stab at his throat. Pivoting, he went for his Colt again, only to have the woman do the most incredible thing: she leaped high into the air and kicked him with her right foot, catching him across the jaw. Pain exploded as she skipped back out of reach.

Fargo collided with someone behind him. A squawk from Sweetpea told him who. Their legs became entangled and down they went. Dreading the sharp slice of steel into his

6

ribs, Fargo shoved clear and rose to his knees. This time he got the Colt out—but there was no one to shoot.

The pair were fleeing across the hurricane deck, the woman helping the man, his arm over her shoulder. Another couple, the two who were admiring the stars, had come running over and were agape with astonishment.

Fargo gave chase. He lost sight of his quarry in the inky shadow of the overhang. He had his choice of right or left and went to the right, to the head of a passageway that ran nearly the entire length of the steamboat. Enough light filtered from the cabins and from the few lamps to reveal there wasn't anyone within fifty feet. Quickly, he turned and flew to the head of the other passageway but the only person close enough was an elderly matron hobbling on a cane.

Fargo had lost them. He ran toward the matron, who drew back as if afraid he was going to attack her. "Did you see two people run past? A man and a woman?"

"The only person I've seen in a hurry is you."

Fargo sprinted on but there was no sign of them. He couldn't understand it. They hadn't had time to get very far. He wondered if they had ducked into one of the forward cabins and retraced his steps, the matron shying away from him as if he were loco.

Around the corner came Sweetpea and the stargazers. Squealing with relief, Sweetpea threw herself at him and hugged him close.

"Skye! Thank goodness you're all right! Who were they? Why were they trying to kill you?"

"I wish to hell I knew."

The other couple, middle-aged and portly, were holding hands. "We couldn't believe our eyes, Maude and me," the man said.

The woman nodded. "Harold and I saw them run at you and that young man draw his knife."

"You got a good look at them?"

"Only a glimpse. They were over in the corner. We thought they were lovers."

Fargo remembered the couple standing cheek to cheek in the shadows. "Why did you say the man was young?" He hadn't been able to tell much, as dark as it was.

"Just an impression I had," Maude answered.

"Were they on the deck before you got there?"

"Now that I think about it," Harold said, "no, they weren't. They showed up just a bit before you did."

Fargo rubbed his sore jaw and pondered. It made no damn sense.

"Maybe they saw you win big at the poker table and were out to help themselves to your poke," Sweetpea said.

"Could be." Fargo had a hunch there was more to it. The pair had been as fiercely intent as starved wolves out to bring down a bull elk.

"Let's hope they don't try again."

"Oh my," Maude declared. "Wouldn't that be positively awful?"

2

Hannibal, Missouri wasn't the sleepy settlement Fargo remembered. It had grown into a bustling town of about three thousand people. Two sawmills provided the lumber for the buildings and sold boatloads more downriver. The four slaughterhouses did the same. Some folks complained about the constant squeals of the hogs being butchered but they were few. To most, those squeals were money in the bank and Hannibal was all about money.

In addition to the sawmills and the slaughterhouses, there were over a dozen general stores—two that sold nothing but hardware—millineries for the ladies, not one but two newspapers, and churches galore. Hannibal had the railroad and a steamboat landing.

It also had, to Fargo's mild surprise, plenty of saloons. From the landing he made straight for the first one he saw, leading the Ovaro by the reins. He'd paid extra to have the stallion brought upriver and he imagined it was as glad as he was to be off the steamboat and to be able to move about again. He looped the reins around a hitch rail and sauntered into a whiskey den that put saloons west of the Mississippi to shame. An ornate mirror ran the length of the back wall. Overhead hung a chandelier that tinkled whenever the front door was opened. The floor was swept clean, the bar polished to a shine. The bartender had muttonchops thick enough to hide in and wore a white shirt with gold suspenders.

Fargo paid for a bottle and retreated to a corner table. He filled his glass and gulped half, and smiled. He was about to gulp the rest when a two-legged mouse in a suit and bowler timidly approached and gave a slight bow. The man had small, deep-set eyes and no chin to speak of.

"Excuse me, but would you be Mr. Fargo?"

"Go away."

"I beg your pardon?"

"Skedaddle. Light a shuck. Leave me be. Scat. Take your pick but do it." Fargo drained the glass.

"You're a bit of a grump."

Fargo refilled the glass and raised it. "Are you still here? You have nuisance written all over you and I want to relax a spell before I go see the gent who sent for me."

"Ah, yes, well." The mouse drew himself up and squared his sloped shoulders. "Permit me to introduce myself. My name is Theodore Pickleman and I was . . ."

In the act of swallowing, Fargo started to laugh and snorted whiskey out his nose. "Damn. Look at what you made me do." He wiped his sleeve across his mouth. "Pickleman?"

"I am afraid so, yes. I'm a lawyer and I've been . . ."

Again Fargo cut him off. "I was right about you. If there are bigger nuisances than lawyers I have yet to meet them. Go away."

"I'm afraid I can't. You see, as I was saying, I represent the Clyborn family and I'm here at the request of the person who wants to hire you."

"Sam Clyborn? Why didn't you say so?" Fargo fished the telegram from his pocket. "I was in Saint Louis when this reached me." He unfolded it and read it again out loud. "Skye Fargo. Urgent you come immediately to Hannibal. Will pay two thousand dollars for your services." He flicked it toward the lawyer. "It's signed Sam Clyborn."

Pickleman picked up the telegram. "I know what it says. I'm the one who sent it."

"How did you know I was in Saint Louis?"

"Sam read in the newspaper about how you were recuperating from a run-in with hostiles. Something about an arrow in your leg."

"I'm fond of Saint Louis," Fargo admitted. "It has almost as many bawdy houses as Denver." He chuckled and downed another half a glass and sat back. "Tell you what. Pull up a chair and you can tell me what Clyborn wants."

"I can't. I'm under strict orders to fetch you straightaway. The *Yancy* was early for once or I'd have caught you at the landing. As it was, a couple named Harold and Maude pointed you out to me as you were going off up the street or I'd have missed you entirely."

"I aim to drink and eat before I go anywhere," Fargo informed him.

Pickleman fidgeted and said, "I am sure Sam will have the cook prepare a meal for you. Bring your bottle if you wish but please accompany me or I will be in hot water."

"You sound scared."

"It's not that so much," the lawyer replied. "But when Sam wants something done, it had better be done the way Sam wants or there is hell to pay."

"Sounds like him and me won't get along," Fargo predicted.

Pickleman uttered a strange sort of bark. "To the contrary. Based on what I've been able to learn about you and your proclivities, I'd say the two of you will hit it off."

"My what?" Fargo seemed to recollect hearing the word before but he would be damned if he could remember when or where.

"Your fondness for whiskey and cards and—how shall I put this?—other things." Pickleman clasped his hands. "Please. I'll beg if I must. I can't afford to have Sam switch to another attorney."

Fargo was loath to go. His stomach was growling and the whiskey they served here was damn good. "You need to learn to stand up for yourself."

"No one stands up to the Clyborns."

"There's more than one?"

"Oh, goodness, yes. There are six now that Thomas Senior has passed on. His wife died years ago. That leaves their four sons and two daughters. Sam is the oldest."

"Didn't I see the name Clyborn on one of the general stores?"

"That you did. Thomas was one of the first to settle here. He saw potential where others saw only wilderness. He realized that where Bear Creek flows into the Mississippi was the perfect spot for riverboats to put in. He started up the first sawmill, and the family still holds a controlling interest. He started up the first slaughterhouse, as well. I daresay half the businesses in Hannibal owe their existence to him."

"So the family is rich?"

"Thomas's net worth when he died was over ten million dollars. Yes, you heard right. *Million.* A sum to stagger the imagination, don't you think?"

It staggered Fargo's. The most he ever had at any time in his life was ten thousand, which he promptly lost in a game of five card stud.

"Now can we go?" Pickleman requested. "I have a carriage waiting. You can tie your horse to the back. The estate is about three miles south of town and we'll want to reach it before nightfall."

"Afraid of the dark, are you?" Fargo poked fun.

"If you read the *Hannibal Journal* you would understand. A scoundrel called Injun Joe has been terrorizing the territory. He is believed to be to blame for several murders and a score of robberies. I wouldn't put it past him to stop our carriage and demand our money."

Fargo patted his Colt. "He's welcome to try."

"Yes, I have heard you are uncommonly quick and accurate. But Injun Joe isn't to be taken lightly. He shows no mercy and he has no remorse or he wouldn't do the horrible deeds he does."

Fargo stood and used his foot to shove his chair back. "You can tell me more on the way out to the Clyborn place."

"You're going then?" Pickleman lit up like a lamp. "I can't thank you enough. I'm in your debt."

Fargo figured he might as well get it over with. He tucked the bottle under his arm and followed the lawyer out. The sun was poised on the western rim of the world and would soon relinquish its reign to the moon. He opened his saddlebags and slid the bottle in while Pickleman impatiently tapped a foot. "Where's this carriage?"

"Down the street."

Fargo unwrapped the reins and followed. It was close to the supper hour. Shops and stores were closing or about to close and people were hurrying home. A lot of them, he noticed, stared at him as they went by. He thought maybe it was his buckskins. Everyone else was wearing either homespun or store-bought clothes. Then he realized he was the only one wearing a six-shooter.

Suddenly a man blocked the lawyer's way. He wore a suit and had a high, wide forehead and a long upturned nose. The lower half of his face was wreathed in a beard as neatly trimmed as Fargo's. "Is it true what I've heard?"

"How can I say when I don't know what it is?" Pickleman responded.

"You know very well what. I find it incredible bordering on the absurd. How could he do such a thing?"

"Now, now. Don't make more of it than there is."

"And don't you make light of it. On second thought, I know perfectly well how he could do it, given his nature."

Fargo said, "Is there a problem?"

"Not at all," Pickleman said. "Where are my manners? Skye Fargo, I'd like you to meet Orion Clemens. He owns the *Hannibal Journal*."

"How do you do?" Clemens offered his hand and looked Fargo up and down. "Fargo, did he say? By your attire I take you for a plainsman." Clemens gave a slight start. "My word.

You're not by any chance the man they call the Trailsman? I've read about you, sir."

"Hell," Fargo said.

Clemens stared down his long nose at the lawyer. "This becomes more interesting by the moment. How does this rather famous gentleman fit into Tom Senior's insane scheme?"

"Insane scheme?" Fargo echoed.

Pickleman waved a hand dismissively. "Pay no attention to our esteemed journalist, Mr. Fargo. He has newspapers to sell, after all." He started to go around but Clemens again blocked his path. "Here now. Out of my way, if you please."

"Be reasonable, Theodore. I owe it to my readers. I already know about the hunt but not the exact rules and who is to oversee it."

"You won't hear them from me." Pickleman glanced about them and lowered his voice. "You're the one who isn't being reasonable. You know very well that an attorney can't violate a client's confidence. I'm sorry but you'll have to dig up your dirt elsewhere." He walked on.

Fargo had caught the one word that might explain why he was sent for. "What was that about a hunt?"

"All in due time, sir."

The carriage was actually a victoria, a luxurious model with a fold-down top and a scalloped floor. The driver wore a purple uniform and a high silk hat. He began to climb down.

"That's all right, James," Pickleman told him. "I'll climb in myself."

Fargo went around to the rear to tie the Ovaro. He wasn't paying attention to the passersby and didn't notice a man come up and stop.

"What's this, then?"

"Hello, Marshal," Pickleman said.

The lawman was broad and square-jawed and wore his badge high on his vest. He wasn't wearing a gun belt but there was a telltale bulge under his left arm. "You didn't answer me." He pointed at Fargo's waist. "Explain to me why your friend is wearing a sidearm in violation of town ordinance?"

"He just got off a steamboat."

"The *Yancy* was the last to dock and that was twenty minutes ago," the lawman said gruffly. "I know every arrival and departure by heart." His tone hardened. "And the firearm ordinance is clearly posted at the wharf."

Pickleman calmly introduced Fargo. "This is Dick Lamar, our marshal. As you can tell, he takes his duties seriously."

"Damn right I do." Lamar held out his hand. "I'll take the Colt, mister. You can have it back when you leave town."

"Sam wouldn't like that," Pickleman said.

"How's that again?"

"Sam Clyborn sent for him. Certainly, take his revolver if you must but don't blame me if Sam wants your head." The lawyer smiled and said not unkindly, "Besides, as you can plainly see, we're on our way out of town anyway so why not let him keep it? He's only here for the weekend. Monday afternoon he is to take a steamboat back down the river to Saint Louis."

This was the first Fargo had heard of working only for two days. Here it was, almost Friday evening. What kind of hunt took that short a time and required someone with his particular skills? There had to be plenty of local hunters who knew the habits of the local wildlife.

Marshal Lamar lowered his hand. "Very well. I'll make an exception but just this once." He stepped up to Pickleman. "Don't think I do it out of fear, either. I'm the one person in Hannibal that Sam can't lord it over and Sam knows it." He wheeled on a boot heel. "Now get the hell out of here before I change my mind."

Pickleman leaned toward Fargo and said quietly, "You must excuse him. He's been at odds with the Clyborn family now and again."

"Why?"

"The marshal lives by the letter of the law and the Cly-borns like to bend the law to suit them. But after all, that's always been a prerogative of the rich and the powerful, hasn't it?"

Fargo didn't answer. He shucked his Henry rifle from the saddle scabbard and climbed into the victoria. There was hardly a speck of dust anywhere and the leather had a nice smell. He settled back with the Henry across his lap.

Pickleman stared at the rifle as if it might bite him. "I honestly doubt you'll have need of your long gun."

"You're the one who said he was worried about Injun Joe," Fargo reminded him.

James cracked his whip. With a slight jounce they were under way. They turned south at the next corner. Beyond the outskirts of town rose a sweep of densely wooded hills.

"I'm only staying the weekend?" Fargo brought up.

"Oh. Yes. I can confirm that much, at least. It's not very long, I grant you, given how far you've come and how much you are being paid. But I think it's safe to say you are in for one of the most interesting experiences of your life."

3

All that was left of the sun was a golden arch. The woods on both sides of the road were mantled in spreading shadows. Soon twilight would descend and they still had miles to go.

Theodore Pickleman was a talker. He prattled on about the glories of Hannibal, about how it was a hub of commerce, how it had grown by bounds the past decade, about the foresight of the man some considered the town's founding father. "Yes, sir. Tom Clyborn was a visionary. He turned that vision into riches most men can only dream of."

Fargo listened with half an ear. He wished he had kept the bottle. He could use a drink. Folding his arm across his chest, he remarked, "Didn't you tell me that creek we crossed is called Bear Creek?"

"Yes. Once these woods teemed with black bears but now there are far fewer." The lawyer gestured at the forest. "Tell me. What do you see?"

Fargo wasn't sure what he was getting at. "Trees?"

Pickleman smiled smugly. "Indeed. You and I see trees. Not Tom Clyborn. He saw black walnut. Hickory. Ash. Sycamores. Maples. An entire logging industry there for the taking."

They had passed logging operations at the outskirts of Hannibal. Trees were being felled at a terrific rate. Fargo couldn't help but reflect that as fast as the forest was being chopped down, in another twenty years there wouldn't hardly be any forest left. He said as much.

"So? That's a long way off. The important thing is that we make money now."

"There's more to life than money."

Pickleman tilted his head and studied Fargo as he might a new kind of bug.

"Don't let Sam hear you say that. To the Clyborns, money is everything. Power. Prestige. Luxury." He patted the victoria's seat. "As you can tell, they only buy the best. Which, by the by, is one of the reasons Sam saw fit to send for you." He paused. "You are widely regarded as being the best there is at what you do. Is that true?"

Fargo shrugged.

"I see. You're not one to brag. But I hope for your sake it is. Sam will be most displeased if you're not all it's claimed you are."

Fargo remembered the comment about a hunt. "Has a bear been acting up? Is that why he sent for me?" So far as he knew, the only other meat-eaters that still roamed these hills and might pose a threat to people were cougars, but cougar attacks were rare.

"Oh, goodness no." Pickleman laughed and shook his head. "You're not here to hunt wild game. Sam sent for you for a special purpose."

Fargo was fed up with being kept in the dark. He fished for information by saying, "Clyborn meant what he said about paying me two thousand dollars?"

"A thousand a day for two days of your time, yes. Not bad when you consider that the yearly income for most people is about five hundred."

The lawyer lapsed into silence, for which Fargo was grateful. He closed his eyes and pulled his hat brim down. A little rest would do him good. He had been up most of the night with Sweetpea. He relived the feel of her lips on his, of her full mounds in his hands, her hard nipples against his palms. He'd like to be with her now, parting those silken thighs of hers and running his hand from her knees to her moist cleft. He felt himself stir and inwardly smiled.

Unexpectedly, the victoria came to a stop.

Fargo opened his eyes. The sun was gone and night was falling. The driver was in the act of lighting the two lamps, one on either side of the seat, that would illuminate their way in the dark.

"Hurry it up, James," Pickleman said. "We don't want to keep Sam Clyborn waiting, do we?"

"No, sir," James replied. He had the first lamp lit and closed the glass. Turning to the second, he opened the glass and bent to light it. In the woods a rifle boomed and the back of the driver's head exploded in a shower of hair and flesh and silk hat.

Fargo was in motion before the sound of the shot died. It had come from the trees to the right; he went left, clearing the seat and the step and landing in a crouch with the victoria between him and the shooter.

Theodore Pickleman was frozen in shock.

"Get down!" Fargo rasped, and when the lawyer didn't move, he reached up and hauled him out of the seat. A second shot blasted and the slug ripped into the victoria inches from his head. Ducking, Fargo turned Pickleman toward the vegetation and gave him a shove.

The lawyer unwittingly straightened and took a step.

Instantly, Fargo grabbed him by the shirt and threw him to the ground. "Are you trying to get yourself shot?" He hunkered beside the rear wheel.

Pickleman didn't move. His mouth worked but no sounds came out. Then he gulped and bleated, "What is going on? Who shot James?"

"How the hell would I know?" Fargo raised his head to peer over the top and nearly lost an ear to a leaden hornet.

Only this time the shot came from a different spot and by the sound was a revolver. He worked the Henry's lever, feeding a cartridge into the chamber.

"This can't be happening. It just can't."

"Tell that to your driver." Fargo risked a look around the rear of the carriage. A black veil had fallen and was rapidly darkening.

Pickleman sat up. "Oh, God. Poor James. I don't understand why anyone would shoot him. He was a good man. He'd never harm a soul."

"They shot him first to keep us here," Fargo guessed. "Now they're waiting for one of us to try and climb up on that seat so they can do the same to us."

"You keep saying *they* but I bet it's only one man. It has to be Injun Joe."

Fargo didn't waste breath explaining. He edged away from the wheel and toward the Ovaro. He was worried the bushwhackers might decide to shoot the horses.

Across the road the undergrowth spouted flame and sound and lead smacked the victoria. Fargo answered in kind, banging off three swift shots. Spinning, he crab-stepped toward the driver's seat. "We have to get out of here," he whispered. "When I climb up, you jump in."

"Not on your life," Pickleman said with a vigorous shake of his head. "We'll be killed before we go ten feet. They can see us but we can't see them."

Fargo remedied that. He shot the lamp. It burst in a shower of flame and whale oil, plunging them in darkness. It also spooked the team. With a strident whinny the near horse bolted and the other horse ran with it. Fargo lunged to try and grab hold of the victoria and swing up but he couldn't get a firm grip and pitched onto his side. The carriage was a score of yards away—and taking the Ovaro with it—before he could get to his knees. "Damn."

"Oh my," Pickleman said.

In the woods a gun thundered.

Fargo saw the muzzle flash. He slammed off two shots while backpedaling. "Hunt cover!" he snapped, and Pickleman scrambled after him.

Across the road both the rifle and the revolver opened up, peppering the undergrowth.

The wide trunk of a maple offered haven. Fargo darted behind it and worked the lever. His elbow bumped the lawyer, who was practically clinging to his back. "When I said to hunt cover I didn't mean *me*."

"Oh, sorry." Pickleman moved a bit back. "It's just that I've never been involved in anything like this before."

Fargo had, more times than he cared to count. "The first rule is don't get shot."

"Am I mistaken or is there more than one shooter?" the lawyer asked.

"The second rule is whisper."

"Oh. Sorry." Pickleman closed his eyes, apparently wrestling with his emotions, and when he opened them he was calmer. He whispered, "There are two of them, am I right?"

"Yes."

"Then it's not Injun Joe. He works alone. But for the life of me, I can't think who else it would be."

"Hush." Fargo was listening. The pair might be stalking them.

The brush remained still, the night quiet, save for the far-off hoot of an owl.

Pickleman didn't stay quiet long. "The Clyborns do have enemies, though. Well, some of the Clyborns do. The youngest, Charlotte, doesn't have any. She's so nice and sweet that everyone in Hannibal adores her."

Fargo looked at him. "There's a third rule to follow."

"There is? What would it be?"

"When I tell you to shut the hell up," Fargo said, "you shut the hell up."

"Oh. Sorry."

Minute after tense minute followed one after the other until fully a quarter of an hour went by. The moon rose above the hills to the east, splashing the woodland with pale light.

"I think they're gone," Pickleman said.

Fargo was beginning to think so, too. Maybe they were afraid the shots would attract others. No sooner did the thought enter his head than hooves thudded out on the road, coming from the south. It was a single horse, coming fast. It stopped a pebble's toss off. "I'll be damned," Fargo said, and grinned.

"What?"

"The best friend I have has four legs."

The Ovaro had either pulled loose of the victoria or the reins had come untied. It stomped a hoof and nickered.

Fargo warily emerged from hiding. Pickleman tried to walk past him and he pushed him back. "The fourth rule is never take anything for granted."

"How many rules are there?"

"The fifth rule is don't ask stupid questions when the man who is trying to save your hide is busy saving it." Fargo patted the Ovaro while probing the undergrowth. Nothing moved. No shots ripped the night. Quickly, he shoved the Henry into the saddle scabbard and forked leather, then reached down. "Come on. We're lighting a shuck."

The lawyer grasped his arm and Fargo swung him up.

"Goodness. I've never ridden double before. Do I hold on to you or the saddle or what?"

Fargo couldn't resist. "What." He reined around and tapped his spurs and brought the Ovaro to a trot. Thanks to the moonlight the road was easy to make out. He stayed in the middle, his hand on the Colt.

"I want to thank you for saving me back there."

"We're not safe yet."

Fargo wasn't convinced they could relax until a mile had fallen behind them. By then he had slowed to spare the Ovaro. As he felt the tension drain from his taut sinews, it suddenly occurred to him that this had been the second attempt on his life in twenty-four hours. There had been the man and woman on the steamboat and now two assassins in the dark of night in the forest. "I wonder," he mused.

"You wonder what?"

"You're going to make some woman a fine wife one day."

Pickleman didn't respond right away. When he did, he chuckled. "Oh. I get it. You're quite the wit. I didn't expect that of you."

"Let me guess. You've taken the notion that my kind must be as dumb as tree stumps."

"I've met very few frontiersmen, Mr. Fargo. Those I have struck me as uncouth louts only interested in three things. Liquor, women, and having a good time."

"That's me, sure enough."

"No, it's not. You might fool others but I suspect there is more to you. Much more."

"If you say so." Fargo rose in the stirrups. He'd heard the drum of hooves. Drawing rein, he waited.

"What are we doing?" Pickleman asked.

"Do you have ears?"

Presently three riders swept into view, riding hard. Fargo swung the Ovaro broadside so they couldn't see his gun hand. It would give him a split-second's advantage, should it come to that.

The three spotted him and slowed. The thick-shouldered man in the lead was holding a rifle and started to raise it but stopped at a bleat of relief from Pickleman.

"Roland? Is that you? Thank God."

"Theodore?" The man gigged his sorrel up close and stopped. "My God, man. What is going on? The carriage came barreling down on us and we stopped it and found James dead. I remembered you had gone into town earlier and came straightaway to find you."

"Highwaymen attacked us," Pickleman said. "Had it not been for Mr. Fargo, here, I would no doubt be as dead as James."

The man turned to Fargo. He had bushy brows and fingers

as thick as spikes and wore a tweed outfit with Hessian boots and a cap. Across his chest was a bandolier of cartridges and on his hip a knife with a stag hilt. "So you're the man Sam sent for? I've heard of you. They say you're one of the best scouts alive."

"I get around," Fargo said.

"Not that it will do you any good this weekend. I know these hills better than anyone."

Pickleman coughed and said, "Mr. Fargo, this is Roland Clyborn, the second of Thomas's four sons. His passion is hunting."

"What was that about this weekend?" Fargo asked.

Roland glanced at the lawyer. "You haven't told him yet?"

"Sam's orders."

"Figures." Roland turned to Fargo. "A word to the wise: Stay out of this. If I were you, I'd turn around and head back to Hannibal and take the first steamboat downriver."

"And if I don't?"

"You will be in trouble up over your head."

4

Someone once told Fargo that rich people were different from ordinary folks. Fargo found the notion preposterous. He'd met enough of the well-to-do to know there were smart ones and dumb ones, gabby ones and quiet ones, nice ones and bastards, generous ones and selfish sons of bitches. The only difference Fargo could see between rich people and ordinary folks was that rich people had more money.

The Clyborns had enough to buy their own state.

Their mansion covered four acres. Patterned after a European manor, it was three stories high. The walls were made of stone taken from a local quarry. A bewildering array of arches and eaves and minarets ran the length of each side. Windows were everywhere: big windows, small windows, square windows, rectangular windows, even a few round ones. A fortune had been spent on the glass alone. Pickleman casually mentioned that the mansion had fifty-seven rooms. Fargo marveled that it wasn't more.

Over a dozen outlying buildings surrounded it. There was a barn, a separate stable for the horses, a blacksmith shop, servants' quarters, a gardener's hut, a woodshed, and more. A quarter-acre of rosebushes was a testament to the money lavished on the grounds.

An army of servants attended to the family's needs. All the male servants wore the same purple uniforms as the dead driver, James. All the maids and cooks and cleaning ladies wore purple dresses that went clear down to their ankles.

Roland Clyborn escorted them back to the carriage. He was quiet on the ride but kept glancing at Fargo as if puzzled by something. The only time he spoke was when Pickleman asked him what he had been doing on the road so late.

"I was on my way to the hunting lodge," Roland replied. "No one has been there in a while and Sam wanted me to be sure the servants have gotten things ready. I don't think it's necessary but Sam never has seen the hired help as entirely reliable."

The two men with him wore purple uniforms. Neither reacted to the insult.

"Is everyone else ready for tomorrow?" the lawyer asked.

"They more or less hate the idea but it's not as if any of us have a choice," Roland responded.

"Don't blame me. All of this was your father's idea and he *was* a tad eccentric."

Roland snorted. "That's a polite way of saying he wasn't sane. But we both know better, don't we? My father was the sanest man alive. He never did anything without a reason."

"True," Pickleman said. "Which makes me believe his motive in this case was to make all of you suffer."

Fargo interrupted with, "Suffer over what?" He figured it had something to do with his being sent for.

"You'll find out soon enough. I don't daresay. Sam has reserved that right."

"And what Sam wants, Sam gets," Roland said.

After that, not a word until they came to the victoria. Roland had stopped the runaways and tied them so they wouldn't go anywhere while he and the servants raced up the road to find out what had happened to Pickleman.

The mansion was half a mile farther.

"How much land does the Clyborn family own?" Fargo asked over his shoulder as the lights came into sight.

Pickleman chuckled. "You've been on Clyborn property since we left Hannibal. Tom Senior laid claim to ten square miles of prime woodland, in addition to his other holdings."

Light lit every window. From a distance it lent the illusion of being a small town.

As soon as they rode up, servants rushed to take their mounts and tend to the carriage. Roland gave orders that the driver's body be carried to the springhouse and wrapped in a blanket until the carpenter could make a coffin.

"You have your own carpenter?" Fargo asked.

"We have our own everything," was Roland's reply.

"Someone will have to inform Marshal Lamar first thing in the morning," Pickleman said.

Roland turned. "What for? His jurisdiction ends at the town limits. The one to report this to is Sheriff Edes."

"I happen to know that the sheriff is off at the capital with his deputy and won't be back for a week to ten days. By then we'll have to bury the body or it will stink to high heaven."

"I don't like involving Marshal Lamar."

"It can't be helped. The murder must be reported," Pickleman insisted.

A gray-haired servant reached for the Ovaro's reins. Fargo motioned him away and said curtly, "No."

The servant looked questioningly at Roland Clyborn.

"Your animal will be taken good care of, I assure you."

"I'll tend to my horse myself."

"That's what the servants are for," Pickleman said. "Why do anything we don't have to?"

"I'm not sure I'm staying." Fargo didn't add that, whether he took the job or not, he intended to track down whoever tried to make worm food of them.

Pickleman's face puckered in worry. "Did I hear correctly? You're thinking of turning Sam down?"

"I haven't heard why I was sent for yet."

"I told you. Sam wants to do that. But you can't have come all this way only to refuse. It would upset Sam terribly."

Fargo looked for a hitch rail but there was none. He led the Ovaro to the base of the mansion steps and let the reins dangle. The stallion was well trained; it wouldn't stray off.

The gray-haired servant had followed him so Fargo made it plain. Patting the saddle, he said, "Anyone touches him, I'll crack their damn skull. Understood?"

Again the servant looked at Roland who motioned. The servant gave a slight bow and walked off.

Fargo shucked the Henry and cradled it in his left elbow.

"You won't need that inside," Pickleman said with an amused twinkle in his eyes.

"It goes where I go."

"I must say," the lawyer remarked. "You're about the most strong-willed person I have ever met, and that includes Tom Senior."

"Follow me," Roland said.

The interior was as lavish as Fargo expected: polished floors, mahogany furniture, paintings, even a few sculptures. The servants who passed them always bowed their heads.

Fargo was led to a sitting room the size of most saloons. Roland indicated a divan and said he would go fetch Sam.

The lawyer began to pace.

"Nerves bothering you?" Fargo asked.

"Sam won't like the attempt on our lives. Not one little bit. And when Sam gets mad—" Pickleman didn't finish.

"I'm not fond of being shot at, myself."

"Highwaymen, I tell you. Everyone knows that road is used almost exclusively by the Clyborns. They figured to kill us and rob us."

Fargo had noticed a portrait. It showed a big man in his fifties or sixties with the same broad shoulders and bushy eyebrows as Roland. The artist had captured the man's piercing gaze and a sense of brooding power. "Thomas Clyborn?"

"Senior, yes. As you can tell, he wasn't a man to be trifled with. Sam is very much the same."

"What about Tom Junior?"

"He's the oldest of the four boys. But how shall I put this?" Pickleman scratched his chin. "Tom the younger isn't exactly a chip off the old block. Fact is, there are some who suspect he's not from the same block at all if you take my meaning."

Before Fargo could reply, into the room swept a force of nature. That was the only way to describe her. She was tall and ravishing, with rich auburn curls, cherry red lips, sharp hazel eyes, and high cheekbones. Her dress had to cost hundreds of dollars. She swept in and stood poised like a monarch about to deliver a speech, those hazel eyes of hers flicking from the lawyer to Fargo and then raking Fargo from his hat to his boots.

Fargo grinned. She was undressing him and studying him and taking his measure all in that one look.

"Samantha!" Pickleman blurted.

It hit Fargo that this was the "Sam" everyone had been talking about. She was as fine a figure of a woman as he ever set eyes on. He caught a whiff of expensive jasmine perfume, and down low, he stirred.

"So you're the famous scout?" Samantha Clyborn asked in a voice as husky as a caress.

"That he is," Pickleman confirmed. "I've brought him from town just as you requested."

Samantha focused on the lawyer. "I didn't *ask* you to bring him. I *told* you to. But I don't recall saying anything about having him shot at."

Pickleman blanched. "Roland told you? Be reasonable, Sam. How was I to know outlaws were lying in wait?"

Roland and others appeared behind her. Since they weren't wearing uniforms Fargo took them to be members of the family.

"Well?" Samantha Clyborn was addressing him. "Are you going to stand there mute or say something?"

"Why did you send for me?"

The vision of loveliness smiled. "Direct and to the point. I like that. I'll answer your question shortly but first there's this business of the attempt on your life."

"Second attempt."

"What?" Samantha said.

"What?" Pickleman echoed.

Briefly, Fargo recited the knife attack by the man and the woman on the steamboat. "I thought they were after my poke but maybe I was wrong and they were after me."

"This is most disturbing," Samantha said. "No one knew I sent for you except for my siblings and Theodore."

"And some of the servants," Pickleman said.

Roland and those with him came up on either side of Samantha. Three of the four were men. All had the same auburn hair and a similar shape to their faces, save one. He was bone thin and had raven black hair and a complexion so pale it gave the impression he hardly ever set foot outdoors.

"Surely you're not suggesting one of us is to blame?" Roland said to Samantha.

"Perhaps one of you thought he would give me an advantage."

The black-haired man stirred. "*You* must think he will, dear sister, or you wouldn't have sent for him."

Samantha regarded him as someone might regard a spider they wanted to step on. "Each of us is allowed a helper, Thomas. Anyone of our choosing, that's how the will reads."

"Yes," Tom said, bobbing his bony chin. "But to send for the likes of him"—he jabbed a finger in Fargo's direction—"Honestly. What can he possibly do that any of our local backwoodsmen couldn't?"

Another of the siblings, whose suit was immaculate and whose every hair was slicked in place and neatly combed, uttered a snort of annoyance. "If anyone has an advantage, it's Roland. He's hunted in the forest since he was a boy. He knows every creek, every nook."

"Stay out of this, Charles," Tom said.

"I will not. I have as much at stake as the rest of you and I think it unfair of Father to choose the method he has. It's absurd."

The last of the brothers, the youngest, cleared his throat.

"I never did understand him. Father had his own ideas and they were never ideas anyone else would have."

"He was a tyrant, Emmett," Tom said. "A petty, mean, miserable, money-pinching goat who—"

Samantha was on him in a long stride. Her hand flashed and the *crack* of the slap was like the crack of a shot. She hit him so hard that Tom rocked on his heels and would have fallen if Charles hadn't caught him. "I'll not have that kind of talk. Do you hear me?"

Tom raised a hand to his red cheek, and glared. "If you ever hit me again, I swear."

"You swear what?"

"Do I really need to spell it out?"

The last of them, the youngest daughter, who by Fargo's reckoning had to be in her early twenties, stepped between Samantha and Tom and cried out, "Enough! Please! Why must you always be at each other's throats? For my sake if for no other reason, try to be nice."

"Nice?" Tom said in contempt.

"Yes, nice," the youngest girl said. "There are people who are, you know. They say nice things and do nice things for other people. I would like, just once, for us to be like them."

"You're a silly dreamer," Tom said. "It's all that reading you do. Readers are always dreamers."

Roland put a hand on the youngest girl's shoulder. "Try not to let them get to you, Charlotte. They've always been this way and they always will."

Tom Junior laughed. "Will you listen to him? You would think he was Sir Galahad but he's no better than the rest of us."

Roland balled his fists. "Have a care, brother."

"Please," Charlotte said.

All of them started to talk at once except for Samantha.

Fargo had listened to enough. He drew his Colt and thumbed back the hammer.

5

The floor was made of maple. Like everything else in the Clyborn mansion, it was a floor only the rich could afford. Fargo didn't give a damn. He pointed his Colt down and banged off a shot that sent slivers flying.

Nearly all of them gave a start. Only Roland, the hunter, who was accustomed to guns going off, and Samantha, didn't jump or flinch.

All eyes swung toward Fargo and the smoke curling from the end of the Colt's barrel. "Now that I've got your attention," he said, and twirled the six-shooter into his holster, "someone better tell me why in hell I'm here or I'm fanning the breeze."

"You have your nerve," Tom Junior said.

"How dare you." From Charles.

"I didn't come all this way to listen to you idiots bicker." Fargo hefted the Henry and turned toward the hall. "For some of us the sun doesn't rise and set with you Clyborns." He took a couple of steps and Samantha's hand enfolded his arm.

"Wait. Please. I'm the one who sent for you and I would like nothing better than to explain why but first I need to have words with my brothers and my sister."

"So long as you're not all day at it."

"It will take far less time than that." Samantha smiled and turned and her smile evaporated. "I want all of you to go to your rooms and wait for me to send for you."

32

"Who do you think you are, our mother?" Tom snapped. "We can do as we damn well please."

"I agree," Charles said. "We're adults, dear sister, not children anymore."

"Then act like adults. Mr. Fargo has come a long way to see me. After I've concluded my business with him, we'll all get together."

"I don't know why you sent for a man like him anyway," Charles said.

"I do," Tom angrily declared. "Our older sister wants to trim the odds so she has a better chance." He wheeled on a shoe heel. "Fine. Let's humor her. By Monday morning all this will be over and none of us need ever listen to her again."

"Unless she wins," Charlotte said.

Tom swore. "Over my dead body."

Charles and Emmett followed them out. Roland lingered to ask, "I'm curious, Sam. What *will* you do if you win?"

"Not now."

"Father left it up to each of us. I know what Charlotte will do. She's too sweet to be selfish. Emmett will probably share, too. Charles, I'm not so sure. As for Tom." Roland stopped and frowned.

"You'll learn my sentiments if and when I claim the prize," Samantha informed him.

Roland nodded at Fargo. "Bringing him in might not help you all that much. You could spend a lot of money for nothing."

"We'll see, won't we?"

Roland left, and Samantha indicated a divan. "Have a seat, why don't you, and I'll explain what this is all about?"

Fargo sank down, draped his arm across the back, and leaned the Henry against his leg. "I could use a drink."

Samantha turned to a pull cord in the corner and gave it a hard yank. Within seconds a maid in a long purple dress appeared and gave another of those bows.

"Yes, ma'am?"

"A glass of whiskey for my guest."

"A bottle," Fargo amended.

"Which brand? We have Early Times, Monumental, and Sour Mash Copper Whiskey, as I recall."

Fargo wasn't particular so long as it went down smooth, but he was fond of Early Times.

"A bottle of Early Times," Samantha told the maid. "You may dispense with a glass."

"Yes, ma'am."

Samantha sat opposite him and folded her hands in her lap, her posture as perfect as posture could be. "Now, then. Suppose we get down to brass tacks. Are there any questions I can answer right off?"

Fargo was honest. He had been thinking of one thing and one thing only since he set eyes on her. "What does it take to get you under the sheets?"

Samantha blinked and her red lips parted. "Mercy me. I don't know whether to be flattered or insulted. What do you take me for, sir? A common trollop?"

"There's nothing common about you. You'd be the queen of any bawdy house you worked at."

Her cheeks blazed red.

"That body of yours is enough to give a man fits," Fargo pressed on. "You must have a list of lovers as long as your arm."

"I'll have you know . . ." Samantha began, and caught herself. The red in her cheeks deepened. "Listen here. I don't know what you are about but it stops this instant. I didn't bring you here to titillate me. I brought you here to help me acquire a fortune."

Fargo put his lust on the back burner of the stove for the time being. "You have my attention."

"Finally." Samantha pointed at the portrait. "My father. A pillar of the community. One of the wealthiest men in all Missouri. He attended church every Sunday without fail."

"You make him sound like a saint."

"I don't mean to." Samantha paused. "The truth is, my father was one of the most coldhearted men to ever draw breath. You can't tell it to look at that painting but he was mean to his core."

Fargo's interest perked.

"He wasn't always that way. Before Charlotte was born, I remember him being just like any other father. He spent most of his time at work but when he was home with us children he was gentle and considerate."

"What changed him?"

"Our mother died giving birth to Charlotte," Samantha revealed. "The whole week after that, Father shut himself in his bedroom and wouldn't come out. When he did, he was a changed man. Something inside him had died. The milk of human kindness, some would call it. From then on he treated us as if we were somehow to blame for Mother's death."

"How old is your little sister?"

"Charlotte is twenty-two. I'm thirty-one. Between us came the four boys. Tom Junior, then Roland, then Charles, and finally Emmett."

"Your father treated all of you bad?"

"Actually, no. He treated Tom even worse. He never said why, but I think it's because he suspected Tom wasn't the fruit of his loins."

"I noticed he doesn't look like any of you," Fargo mentioned.

"It soured our father on us even more. Our entire lives were spent under his heel. One evening at supper some months ago, he told us that we were vultures waiting around for him to die. He said he was glad none of us had given him grandchildren because they would be vultures, too."

"How many of you are married?"

"None of us."

That struck Fargo has peculiar. "There's six of you and not one has ever had a hankering for a hearth and home?" He didn't, but then he wasn't like most people. His wanderlust was too strong. It would be years, if ever, before he was willing to give up the saddle for a rocking chair.

"I can't speak for the others but I've just never met the right man." Samantha frowned. "In a way I'm glad. Our father grew to hate children. Not just his own but *all* children. They reminded him of our mother. They reminded him of his loss. Grandchildren would be more reminders."

Fargo regarded the portrait in a whole new light. "From what you're telling me, your father sure was a son of a bitch."

"You have no idea. He did all he could to make our lives miserable. I could recite you a list as long as your arm." Sam stopped. "One incident should suffice. Roland met a woman once and was thinking about marrying her. Do you know what our father did? He drove a wedge between them. Insulted and belittled the poor woman until she wouldn't have anything to do with us and broke up with my brother."

Fargo's estimation of Roland rose several notches.

"Then there's poor Charlotte. She fell in love only a year ago or so. Our father had her beau investigated and one evening had him invited to supper with the rest of us and then proceeded to inform Charlotte that the man she had given her heart to was in fact seeing another woman behind her back. It broke her heart."

"He ever do anything to you?"

"All sorts of things I refuse to talk about. But the worst of his spite was reserved for Tom. He was convinced Mother had slept with someone else even though she had insisted she hadn't. Father always called Tom his 'little bastard.' Father insulted him mercilessly, and always went on about what he saw as Tom's many flaws. I tell you, it got so bad, many was the time I cringed inside at how terribly Father was treating him."

"How did your brother take it?"

"You saw him. He hates Father for the abuse he suffered and he hates us for not defending him."

"What about Charles and Emmett?"

"Charles avoided Father as much as possible. He spends most of his time at the men's club in town. He hardly ever associates with women. As for Emmett, he's young yet, like Charlotte, and just as innocent."

"That leaves you."

"I'm the oldest. I have a sense of responsibility. I've always felt I needed to look after them and protect them. I admit I didn't do enough to help Tom but there wasn't much I *could* do given how much Father hated him. I devoted myself to running the household and spent all my nights alone in my room."

Fargo had one last question. "Why have you told me all this?"

Samantha smoothed her dress, which clung enticingly to her thighs. "I want you to fully understand what you are getting yourself into. I want you prepared for what is to come. Which brings us to why I sent for you."

At last, Fargo thought.

Just then an older male servant entered and bowed. "Begging your pardon, ma'am, but I thought you should know."

"What is it, Jarvis? I'd rather not be disturbed right now."

"It's this gentleman's horse." Jarvis nodded at Fargo.

"What about it?"

"I was outside when he told everyone not to touch it."

"And?" Samantha said impatiently.

"Your brother, Tom, saw it out front and is having it taken to the stable even as I speak."

Fargo was off the divan in long strides. Samantha called for him to wait but he shouldered past Jarvis and hurried down the hall to the front door. Throwing it open, he stepped outside. At the bottom of the steps stood Tom Clyborn, watching a servant lead the Ovaro off by the reins.

Fargo went down the steps three at a bound. His jingling spurs alerted Tom who turned just as he reached him. Without saying a word, without any warning whatsoever, Fargo hit him flush on the jaw.

Down Tom went. More stunned than hurt, he rubbed his chin and looked up in anger. "What the hell?"

"Don't ever touch a man's horse without his say-so." Fargo strode past him and bellowed at the servant, "Hold it right there."

The servant stopped and looked back.

"Let go of him."

The servant quickly did and retreated. "I was only doing what I was told, mister."

"That's the only reason I don't bust your skull." Fargo snatched the reins. West of the Mississippi, taking a man's horse for any reason was a hanging offense. "Tell the rest that no one goes near my horse but me. Savvy?"

"Yes, sir."

"Then make yourself scarce." Fargo slid the Henry into the saddle scabbard and patted the stallion's neck. "If I am touchy about anything, I am touchy about you."

"How dare you?" Tom Clyborn was livid with wrath. His hands were clenched so tight his knuckles were white. "No one strikes me with impunity. Do you hear me? No one."

"I made it plain my horse wasn't to be moved."

"This is *our* estate. *We* say what will and won't be done. If I want to put your damn animal in the stable, I by God will!"

Fargo placed his hand on his Colt. "Care to bet?"

"You're threatening me? On my own land? In front of the servants?" Tom shook with fury. "You miserable lout. You've just made the worst mistake of your life."

"I've tangled with Apaches and Comanches," Fargo said.

"What do a bunch of stinking red savages have to do with this?"

"Compared to them, as threats go, you're downright puny."

Tom's face twitched and he raised his fist but a jasmine-wreathed vision slipped between them and placed a hand on his chest.

"That will be enough," Samantha said.

"He struck me."

"Let it pass."

"Like hell." Tom glowered over her shoulder at Fargo. "Mark my words, plainsman. You have made a mortal enemy this day." Whirling, he stormed toward the house. Two servants scurried out of his path but one wasn't fast enough and was shoved aside. Another moment, and Tom slammed the front door behind him.

"That was unfortunate," Samantha said.

"Forget about him," Fargo said. "I'm not waiting another minute for you to tell me why you've sent for me."

"Certainly." Samantha smiled. "I want you to be my partner in a hunt unlike any other. There's just one catch." Her smile faded. "I can't guarantee we'll live through it."

6

The twenty riders wound along a pockmarked trail that was taking them steadily deeper into the lush green forest. High above, the morning sun blazed bright. Around them, songbirds warbled and squirrels scampered.

It was as perfect as a day could be, but Skye Fargo didn't let it lull him into letting his guard down. Not when there had been two attempts on his life.

A monarch butterfly flitted past. Fargo watched it, envying it its freedom. Arching his back, he stretched and breathed deep of the rich wood scent. He wished he was back in the Rocky Mountains.

Hooves thudded, and Charles Clyborn came up next to him. "Good morning. We hadn't had a chance to talk yet and I thought this an excellent opportunity." As usual, Charles was immaculately dressed, this time in a riding outfit that was the pinnacle of fashion.

"Did you, now?"

"I'm sorry. Am I bothering you? I only wanted to make your acquaintance." Charles smiled. "Frankly, I'm surprised you're still here. I understand my sister explained everything."

"She's paying me a thousand dollars a day."

"Ah. To you I suppose that's a lot of money. Even so,"— and Charles's smile became a frown—"do you have any idea what you have let yourself in for?"

"A hunt, she called it."

"She told you all the rest? How this was our father's bi-

40

zarre idea? How he refused to leave each of us an inheritance, as any reasonable person would have done? No, that wasn't good enough for him. Or I should say it wasn't vicious enough. So he concocted this ridiculous contest where we must pit ourselves against each another."

"It's mighty unusual," Fargo conceded. Which was putting it mildly. According to the will, only one of Clyborn's children could inherit his enormous wealth and vast holdings. It would all go to whoever won a special hunt. "How far is it to this hunting lodge of yours?"

"As the crow flies, the lodge is about twelve miles from the mansion. Since we left at seven we should be there by noon at the very latest." Charles sniffed. "I have only ever been there a few times. I am not the hunter Roland is. With him it's a passion. I've never liked the sight of blood or seeing animals suffer."

"They don't if you drop them with one shot."

"You sound like Roland. Me, I would much rather enjoy the comforts of my club. A fine dinner with friends, a friendly game of cards or perhaps chess, a glass or three of vintage port, and intelligent conversation." Charles gazed about with distaste. "The wilds are not to my liking. The sun burns my skin and the plants makes me itch and don't get me started on the mosquitoes and other bugs."

"You're a city boy at heart."

"I freely admit it, yes. My life would be complete if Father had left me a paltry million or two. I could spend the rest of my days doing what I love best. But he hated me as much as he hated the rest and he refused my request." Charles glanced back. "Well, if you'll excuse me, I shouldn't leave my partner alone too long. He hates the wilds as much as I do." Reining around, Charles rode back down the line.

As Fargo understood the rules, each of them was allowed to have one person help them in the hunt. Samantha had sent for him. Charles had picked a friend from his club. Charlotte chose a female cousin about her age. Emmett had a friend from town. Tom's partner was a sullen, hulking backwoodsman. Roland was the only one who intended to hunt alone.

Hooves drummed again, and Samantha took Charles's place at Fargo's side. "What were the two of you talking about just now?"

"How much your brother loves the outdoors."

Samantha was wearing a blue riding habit with buttons up the front and a full skirt. The jacket had white at the collar and white at the ends of the sleeves. She had put her hair up in back, and her top hat was tipped forward. She also wore doeskin gloves and had a riding crop in her left hand. "Charles has disliked nature ever since he was seven and he was bitten by a garter snake."

"That outfit fits you real nice."

"Don't start. I rebuffed your advances yesterday and I will rebuff them today." Samantha smiled thinly. "I'm well aware of your reputation, Mr. Fargo. It's claimed that you have bedded more women than Casanova."

"Who?"

"A great lover. It is alleged that he made love to over a thousand in his lifetime."

"That's all?"

For the first time since Fargo met her, Samantha Clyborn laughed. "Humility is not one of your traits, I see. But I must admit there are moments when you amuse me."

Fargo leaned toward her and raked her body with a hungry stare that left no doubt as to his meaning when he said, "I can do a lot more than that."

"Honestly." Samantha shook her head. "You never give up, do you? What will it take to get it through your head that I'm not the least bit interested?"

"I know better."

"Don't flatter yourself. If I have refused myself male companionship all these years, why would I possibly indulge in a dalliance with you, of all people?"

"Because there are no strings attached," Fargo answered

truthfully. "We do it and that's it. You'll never see me again after this weekend is over and I'll never tell a soul you indulged."

"That's hardly sufficient cause. Can't you think of anything better?" she mockingly asked.

"I can think of one thing."

"What would that be?"

"The feeling you get when you gush."

Samantha jerked her head back as if he had slapped her. "I daresay you are the most brazen man I've ever met. You have no respect for a lady."

"I have plenty of respect," Fargo disagreed. "I also know something about ladies that most men don't."

"Oh? And what would that be?"

"A lady will part her legs just like any other woman if she is interested enough."

"I should slap you."

"I'd slap you back."

Samantha's eyes blazed with anger. "You're the most aggravating man I've ever met and that includes my father." Reining sharply around, she jabbed her heels.

Fargo chuckled. He had planted the seed. Now all he could do was wait and see if it took root. On a whim he jabbed his own heels and rode to the head of the line. "Mind some company?"

Roland was in the lead. He wore the same tweed hunting garb as the day before, and in addition to the stag-hilted hunting knife he had a Smith and Wesson revolver on his other hip. "Not at all. Out of all of them, you're the only one I have anything in common with."

"I wanted to ask. Why didn't you pick a partner like the rest?"

"No need," Roland said. "I've hunted every square foot of this forest. An exaggeration, perhaps, but not by much. Whatever we're to hunt down, I'm confident I'll win the inheritance."

"No one knows what it is?"

Roland shook his head. "It's a condition of the will. Pickleman is to read the clause that explains everything this evening after supper. All we know is that my father called it a hunt."

Fargo was surprised by what he said next.

"I'd never admit this to my brothers or sisters, but the reason I've spent so much time in the woods was to get away from my father and to get away from them. Father, with his carping and his insults. My siblings, with their never-ending bickering. It got so, I spent more of my time at the hunting lodge than I did at the mansion."

"You like killing game?" Fargo had met some who lived for the thrill of the chase and the blood of the shot.

"I don't kill just to kill, if that's what you're getting at. I hunt for food. That might sound silly given how well-off we are but I'd rather eat venison than beef any day, and the butcher doesn't carry bear meat."

"What will you do if you end up with all your father's money?"

"Give shares to my brothers and sisters. It's only right, the hell we've endured. The rest I'll sock away in a bank and live pretty much as I have been all these years. I don't care about controlling everyone, like Sam does. Or only wearing the best clothes and being a member of the most expensive men's club in Hannibal, as Charles does. To me the forest has always been enough."

Fargo decided he liked this man. "I hope you win."

Roland shifted and gazed down the line. "Don't let Sam hear you say that or she's liable to take her riding crop to your head." He grinned as he said it but he was serious.

"Everyone keeps saying how mean she is but I've yet to see it," Fargo mentioned.

"It's not that she's mean so much as she is controlling. She loves being in charge, and woe to anyone who bucks her."

"I can take care of myself."

"No doubt you can in the mountains and on the prairie. But this is Missouri, and Sam is a power to be reckoned with. If she wanted, she could have you arrested and the key thrown away."

"On what charge?" Fargo skeptically asked.

"Take your pick. Right now you're in her good graces but whatever you do don't cross her."

On that dire note Fargo fell back in line. He kept to himself for the next couple of hours. The humidity got to him but for the most part he enjoyed the Missouri woods as much as he would any other.

In addition to bear and deer, Missouri was home to elk and—or so he had heard—a few moose. The streams and rivers were favorite haunts of beaver and muskrat while woodchucks were the bane of many a farmer. Smaller game like rabbits, foxes, and raccoons were everywhere. The day sky was ruled by eagles and hawks, the night sky by owls and bats. Catfish and carp were fished out of deep pools while bass thrived in the ponds and lakes and trout ran the swifter waterways.

Fargo could see why Roland liked it here so much. There was plenty of animal sign for those who knew how to read it.

Their little caravan stopped about midmorning to rest the horses. Roland called a halt in a clearing and Fargo dismounted to stretch his legs. He had taken only a few steps when a petite bundle of winsome legs and young innocence imitated his shadow.

"Can we talk, Mr. Fargo?" Charlotte asked.

"I'm right popular today."

"It's about my sister."

"What about her?" Fargo figured either Samantha had told her of his remarks about ladies spreading their legs or Samantha was having second thoughts about hiring him.

"What have you done to her?"

"Not a damn thing. Why? What did she say?"

"She confided in me that she thinks you are just about the most interesting man she ever met."

"Are you sure she was talking about me?"

"Yes, indeed." Charlotte bobbed her chin and her lustrous hair bobbed with it. She put her hands on her slim waist and squared her shoulders, which had the effect of thrusting her bosom against her dress. "I've never heard her say the flattering things about any man that she does about you."

"You must have heard wrong."

"No, I did not. It only came up because I happened to mention I think you are uncommonly handsome and she—"

"You do?" Fargo interrupted, and smiled. "I happen to think that you're uncommonly handsome, too."

"Honestly, Mr. Fargo," Charlotte said in mild exasperation. "Women aren't handsome. They're beautiful or lovely or pretty."

"You're all of that, too." Fargo bent close to her ear. "You remind me of a ripe cherry in a cherry tree."

"I do?"

"I want to pluck you and eat you."

Charlotte gasped and put a hand to her throat. "Mr. Fargo! The things that come out of your mouth."

Fargo stared at her bosom. "It's the things that go into my mouth that I'm fond of."

"Surely you can't mean—" Charlotte stopped and flushed a vivid scarlet. "You are scandalous, sir. How can you talk about me this way when I've just told you that my sister thinks so highly of you?"

"I like greener pastures as much as the next hombre."

Charlotte's brow furrowed in confusion. "I have no idea what you're talking about, and quite frankly, I don't think I want to." She peered at his face as if trying to see through him. "If I didn't know better, I'd swear you are undressing me with your eyes."

"I am," Fargo said with a grin, "and I like what I see."

"Well, I never." Charlotte turned and said over her shoulder. "I will keep this between us to spare Sam. But if you ever talk to me like this again, I'll slap your face."

"That's fine by me."

"It is?"

"I like it rough." Fargo smothered a laugh at her shock and hasty departure.

Two seeds planted, he thought to himself. He gazed at the ring of trees and noticed the glint of the sun off of metal a score of yards into the undergrowth. One of their servants, he reckoned. But glancing about, he realized that everyone was accounted for.

The next instant a shot blasted.

7

After the two attempts on his life Fargo took it for granted this was the third. As the shot shattered the muggy Missouri air, he dived flat. He didn't feel the searing pain of lead ripping through him and thought the shooter had missed. Then he glanced up.

Emmett Clyborn had a hole in the center of his forehead and an even bigger hole on the back of his head where the slug had burst out. He was swaying, his eyes wide with shock. Many of the others were gaping at him in stunned disbelief.

"Get down!" Fargo bellowed.

A second shot cracked.

Charles Clyborn had started to duck and his hat went flying. He dropped flat just as a third shot rang out but the third one didn't come from the woods; Roland Clyborn was shooting back.

Fargo whipped out his Colt and added to the hail. He fired at where he had seen the gleam of metal, two swift shots, and then he was up and running toward the woods, zigzagging to make it harder for the shooter to hit him. Roland ran with him and together they charged toward where tendrils of gun smoke hung in the air.

"Where?" Roland roared, turning right and left.

Fargo spied movement off through the trees. "There!" He pointed and weaved among the boles on the fly. All he wanted was one clear shot. Just one. The crash of the undergrowth and the hammer of hooves told him he wasn't going to get it.

In anger he snapped off a shot in the direction of the sounds and came to a stop. The hoofbeats rapidly faded.

"We should go after him!" Roland fumed.

"And leave the others?" Fargo shook his head. Especially since in both previous tries on his life there had been two would-be assassins, not one. Which begged the question: Where was the other one?

Roland jerked his Spencer rifle to his shoulder but he didn't fire. With an oath he jerked it down again, then said in horror, "Emmett!" Wheeling, he raced for the clearing.

Fargo followed, watching both their backs.

Everyone was gathered around the body. Charlotte was on her knees, clutching Emmett's limp hand and bawling hysterically. Samantha was seeking to comfort her. Charles and Tom appeared to be in shock. Pickleman was as pale as a bedsheet. The servants were staying respectfully back and whispering among themselves.

Out of all of them only one person didn't appear the least bit upset—the backwoodsman Tom had picked as his partner. The man was picking at his teeth with a fingernail.

"Who would do this?" Charles said, aghast. "Why kill poor Emmett?"

Fargo was scanning the woods. That the second assassin hadn't opened up on them didn't mean he wasn't out there. Or did it? A disturbing thought struck him, a thought he kept to himself. He did say, "We can't stand around in the open like this. We're sitting ducks."

Some of the others gave him angry looks.

"He's right," Roland said. "We should make haste to the lodge. We don't know but whoever did this might come back."

Samantha had an arm around Charlotte and was saying, "There, there. You need to calm down. You need to control yourself."

The younger woman's face contorted in disbelief. *"Calm? How can any of us be calm at a time like this? Emmett is dead."*

"I know that, dear," Samantha responded, "and I don't want any of the rest of us to share his fate. Please. We must collect our wits and get out of here."

It was done quickly. Servants were directed to wrap Emmett in a blanket and drape him over his horse. Fargo was going to take hold of the reins but Tom snatched them before anyone else could.

They pushed hard. Every moment was an eternity of suspense. They never knew but when another shot might thunder and another of them might wind up wrapped in a blanket.

Fargo had time to think and came to several conclusions. Again, he kept them to himself. They had gone about a mile when he slowed and let some of the others pass him so he could rein alongside Tom. On the other side of him was the hulking backwoodsman. "I'm sorry about your brother."

Tom glanced at the horse he was leading, and the body. "Whoever killed him will pay. Mark my words."

"Any idea who it could be?"

"How would I know?" Tom snapped. "It's not as if we haven't made enemies. When you're rich and powerful you can't help stepping on toes."

"So you think it's someone with a grudge against your family?"

"What else?"

Fargo didn't answer. Instead he said, "Your friend, there, didn't seem bothered."

The backwoodsman had been gazing into the forest but now he turned his craggy face and gave Fargo a withering look. "You talkin' about me, mister? 'Cause if you are, I ain't Mr. Tom's friend. I hardly know him. I hardly know any of them." He motioned at the family members up ahead. "So no, it doesn't bother me a lick that one of them was shot."

"Must you be so cold about it?" Tom demanded. To Fargo he said, "This is Cletus Brun. He's about the best hunter in Hannibal, next to Roland. I'm paying him for his services this weekend just as my sister is paying you."

Brun snorted. "Shucks. Your brother ain't all that great. I beat him once out to the fair in the turkey shoot."

"Don't underestimate him," Tom warned.

"Don't you underestimate me," Brun said.

"Whoever shot Emmett and almost shot Charles is bound to try again," Fargo mentioned.

"Have you ever been to our lodge?" Tom asked, and answered his own question. "No, of course you haven't. It's a fortress. We'll be safe there."

"For how long?"

Tom didn't hide his annoyance. "Why are you bringing this up? To upset me? Isn't it bad enough I've lost one of my brothers? Must you rub my nose in the fact I might lose more of my family?"

"So you really care about them?"

"Go away," Tom said. "I didn't like you when we first met and I like you less now. So what if I haven't gotten along with them in the past? They're still my brothers and sisters."

Cletus Brun said, "You heard Mr. Tom. Go pester someone else, little man, and leave us be."

Fargo couldn't remember the last time anyone called him "little." But the woodsman was a lot wider across the chest and shoulders and must outweigh him by sixty to seventy pounds. "Suit yourselves." He tapped his spurs and rode to the head of the line.

Roland was a study in glum. "I just don't get it," he said as Fargo came up. "I just don't get it at all."

"Get what?"

"Why the killer chose Emmett. He could have shot any of us. Why Emmett? Emmett was just a kid."

"He also shot at Charles."

Roland gave a start. "The next oldest. It's almost as if the killer started with the youngest and was working his way up."

Fargo hadn't thought of that. "How long until we reach the hunting lodge?"

"Another hour and a half yet, maybe more. Why?"

They were about to go around a bend in the trail.

"Keep going," Fargo said. "I'll catch up." He rode past the bend and promptly reined into the woods. A dozen yards in he drew rein. No one else had seen him break away. He sat and watched them file by, one by one until the last of the pack animals went past.

Fargo was alone. Silence fell but it didn't last long. A jay shrieked and a robin broke into song and presently a doe and a fawn emerged from the greenery and crossed the trail farther down.

Fargo was acting on another hunch. Odds were, whoever shot Emmett wanted to add to the tally, in which case the killer might be stalking them. He stayed where he was as the minutes crawled on turtle's feet. He was about convinced he had been wrong and was raising the reins when the Ovaro pricked its ears and turned its head toward the trail.

Around the bend came a rider. A middle-aged man of middling height who looked as if he never bathed and wore clothes that looked as if they had never been washed. He was chewing lustily and his cheek bulged, and a moment later he spat tobacco juice. He held a rifle by the barrel, the stock propped on his thigh.

This, then, was the killer. Fargo let him go by. He mentally counted to thirty, reined to the trail, and shadowed the shadower.

Fargo could have shot him. He could ambush him as the killer had ambushed them but he needed answers and the only way to get them was to take him alive.

Spitting tobacco every now and again, the man rode along as if he didn't have a care in the world.

Fargo stayed well back. At each turn he slowed and checked before riding on. A quarter of an hour went by. Half an hour. More. By Fargo's reckoning they were near the hunting lodge. At the next bend he slowed again and warily risked a peek.

The man had stopped. Thirty yards away he sat his horse

in the middle of the trail. For a few moments Fargo thought the man had heard him. Then it hit him—the killer was waiting for someone.

Reaching down, Fargo shucked the Henry. He quietly ratcheted a round into the chamber and swung down. Holding on to the reins, he led the Ovaro in among some oaks and tied the reins to a limb. Then, paralleling the trail, he crept forward. The killer had his back to him. It would be so easy to fix a bead between his shoulder blades and bring him crashing down.

The man's sorrel stamped and the man twisted in the saddle.

Fargo froze. He was in a crouch in high weeds and hoped he blended in.

The man was staring back down the trail and had his head cocked to one side.

A second later Fargo heard the thud of hooves.

Around the bend came two more on horseback, a man and a woman. Both were young, no older than twenty-five, and wore matching riding outfits and polished boots. Both had brown hair and brown eyes. Both had oval faces, thin eyebrows and thin lips. Judging by how much alike they looked, Fargo took them for brother and sister. Neither wore a revolver that he could see, but from the saddle scabbard on each horse jutted the hardwood stock of a rifle.

Tobacco Man didn't seem surprised or alarmed. He turned his mount sideways and leveled his Spencer and when they were ten feet out he said, "That's close enough."

The pair came to a stop. They glanced at one another and smiled.

"What's so funny?" Tobacco Man demanded.

"We thought we made our wishes clear back in Hannibal, monsieur," the young man said with an accent that made Fargo think of New Orleans, and the French Quarter.

"We told you that you were not to take a hand in this yet here you are," the young woman chimed in.

Tobacco Man showed his yellow teeth in a sneer of contempt. "And I told you two that I don't scare easy. You're the ones who should stay out of it if you know what's good for you."

"We can't do that," the young man said.

"We've been paid," the young woman said.

"So have me and my pard," Tobacco Man said. "The difference being that one of us is on the inside, which gives us an edge." He wagged the Spencer. "Were I you I'd light a shuck and forget this whole business."

"We can't do that," the young man said again.

"A contract is a contract," said the young woman.

"You two are damned peculiar. You dress alike and you talk alike and I suspect you even think alike. It's spooky."

"Do you hear him, sister?"

"I hear him, brother."

They laughed.

"That's exactly what I'm talkin' about," Tobacco Man said. "Now get it through your heads that this is our job, not yours. My partner and me are locals. You two are from out of town. That gives him and me a better right."

The young man put his left hand on his saddle horn and lowered his other hand to his side. "What a marvelous convolution of logic."

"Isn't it though?" his sister agreed.

"A what?" Tobacco Man said.

"When we saw you following Charles Clyborn around Hannibal we knew you were a competitor," the brother said.

"We're not being paid for you or your friend so we tried to persuade you and your friend to bow out," added his sister.

Tobacco Man spat dark juice.

"It didn't work," the brother declared.

"No, it didn't," the sister echoed.

"So now you leave us no choice."

"None at all."

Tobacco Man raised his Spencer. "You prattle worse than

biddy hens, the pair of you. Since you won't listen, you're the ones who leave me no choice. I'll shoot you both dead if you don't light a shuck. Be smart and make yourselves scarce in these parts."

Once again the brother and sister glanced at one another and then at Tobacco Man.

"Did you know when you woke up this morning?" the brother asked.

"Did you feel it in any way?" from the sister.

"Know what?" Tobacco Man responded.

It was the sister who said, "Did you know that this was the day you were going to die?"

8

Fargo had stayed still and listened in the hope of learning who was behind the attempts on his life and the death of Emmett Clyborn. He suspected that the brother and sister were the same pair who attacked him on the *Yancy*. He hadn't gotten a good look at their faces but it had to be them.

Suddenly the brother's arm swept up and cold steel streaked from his hand.

Tobacco Man jerked the Spencer but he was much too slow. The knife caught him in the throat and blood burst in a geyser. Crying out, Tobacco Man clutched at the knife, only to have more scarlet spray from between his fingers. Somehow he stayed in the saddle and tenaciously tried to bring the Spencer to bear.

Fargo started to rise. He saw what happened next and could hardly credit his eyes.

The sister swung her horse in close to Tobacco Man's. Placing both hands on the saddle, she whipped her leg up and around. Her foot caught Tobacco Man under the jaw and snapped his head back with an audible *crack*. She was so quick her leg was a blur.

Fargo had never seen the like. He charged onto the trail and raised the Henry but brother and sister were already flying into the trees. The sister looked back and saw him, and grinned. Fargo took aim, only to have the vegetation close around them before he could shoot. "Damn it." He ran to

Tobacco Man, who had toppled from the saddle and lay on his side, convulsing. A crimson pool was forming under him.

Kneeling, Fargo said, "Can you hear me? Can you talk?"

Tobacco Man went on quaking and shaking.

"It was you who shot Emmett, wasn't it?" Fargo gripped his arm. "Who hired you and your partner?"

A strangled whine issued from Tobacco Man's ravaged throat. He tried to speak but all that came out of his mouth was more blood.

"Who hired you?" Fargo asked again, and shook him.

The man looked up. His mouth moved but all he uttered were moans. Abruptly arching into a bow, Tobacco Man gave a last gasp and was still.

Fargo rose and kicked the ground. If not for the brother and sister, he would have had the information he wanted. He supposed he should be glad that one of the killers had been disposed of but he would much rather know who was behind it.

Once again hooves pounded and Fargo turned up the trail as Samantha and Charles Clyborn and two servants trotted into sight. They didn't draw rein until they were practically on top of him.

"Who's that?" were the first words out of Charles's mouth.

"The man who shot your brother."

Charles bent low. "I have a feeling I should know him from somewhere but I can't remember where."

"Of course you should," Samantha said. "He lives on the outskirts of Hannibal. His name is Bucklin Anders. He got into trouble for poaching. The *Hannibal Journal* had the story."

"That was over a year ago," Charles marveled. "How can you remember something so unimportant from that far back?"

"I remember everything."

Charles turned to Fargo. "Congratulations. You've avenged my brother and saved the rest of us from a bullet in the back. You have my deepest gratitude."

"Mine as well," Samantha said.

Fargo started to tell them that he hadn't killed Anders, that it had been the brother and sister who tried to kill him on the steamboat. But he didn't. For a reason that even he couldn't explain, he decided not to. Instead he said, "You came back to find me?"

Samantha nodded. "I noticed you were missing and asked Roland where you got to. He told me about you riding off the trail. It wasn't hard to deduce what you were up to."

"You took a risk riding back." Fargo smiled up at her. "I didn't know you cared all that much."

"Don't flatter yourself." Samantha gave orders to the servants and they climbed down to tend to the body.

Fargo put a hand on her leg. "I'd like to repay you for being so concerned about me."

"You're incorrigible." Samantha sniffed. "And I'll thank you to take your fingers off my person."

Chuckling, Fargo did as he was bid but he contrived to run his hand from her knee to her ankle before doing so. "Nice dress," he said.

"I should shoot you."

"I can't help you in the hunt if I'm dead."

Despite herself, Samantha chuckled. "I'm beginning to regret sending for you. Your reputation as a woman-chaser doesn't do you justice. You're worse than that. You're a satyr. Part randy man and part randy goat."

Charles had climbed down and was going through Bucklin Anders's pockets. "My Lord, this man stinks. Didn't he ever hear of lye soap and water?" He found a cowhide poke and opened the drawstring. "Will you look at this? There must be five hundred dollars or better."

"Blood money," Samantha guessed.

"He have any friends that you know of?" Fargo asked.

"I never met the man so I couldn't say."

"I have no doubt that if he did they are as big an offense to the human nose as he was," Charles said. He pulled a handkerchief out and covered the lower half of his face. "This is the first instance I've come across where a man smells worse before he's buried than he will after."

"Quit exaggerating," Samantha chided.

Fargo headed back down the trail to claim the Ovaro. The shadow he acquired this time had four legs and a tail with a lovely in blue on top. "Want something?"

"Can I trust you, Mr. Fargo?"

"Yes and no."

"I'm serious."

Fargo stopped and looked up at her. He had to squint against the glare of the sun. "So am I. Yes, you can trust me to do the best I can to help you in the hunt. No, you can't trust me if we're alone tonight."

Samantha let out a sigh. "You never give up, do you? You latch on to a woman and pester her until she gives in."

"No. I let her know I'm interested. The rest is up to her."

"I've made it as plain as plain can be that I'm not interested. Why, then, do you persist in your advances?"

"I don't believe you."

"You're saying I don't know my own mind?"

"I think you really want me but you're pretending you don't because that's what you think a real lady would do."

Lightning bolts danced in Samantha's eyes. "Are you suggesting I'm *not* a lady?"

"You're as ladylike as they come," Fargo admitted. "Wanting a man doesn't make you less of one. It makes you a woman."

"Pardon my language but you confuse the hell out of me."

"Good." Fargo grinned and went into the woods. He unwrapped the reins from the oak branch and stepped into the stirrups. Truth to tell, he was enjoying his cat and mouse with Samantha. The more she resisted, the more he craved her. Something told him that if she gave in, he would be in for the time of his life.

Roland had stopped the caravan to wait for them. He told

Fargo that he had wanted to come look for him but Samantha insisted he stay with the others. They got under way, and no sooner did Fargo rein into line than Tom and Cletus Brun were next to him.

"I hear you killed the man who shot my brother," Tom said.

"His name was Anders," Fargo hedged, and made it a point to glance out the corner of his eye at Cletus Brun. Sure enough, a scowl rippled across the hulking Missourian's craggy face. "Ever hear of him?"

"Can't say that I have, no."

"How about your friend there?"

Brun's head swiveled on a neck as thick as a bull's. "I told you I'm not his friend. And I never heard of anyone called Anders, either."

"He was a local."

"So? I don't know everybody in Hannibal," Brun rumbled. "I keep to myself. I don't like people all that much."

"He was a hunter like you."

"I just told you I didn't know him. Are you calling me a liar?"

Fargo figured that now was as good a time as any to test his newest hunch. Casually placing his hand on his Colt, he said simply, "Yes."

"Here now," Tom said.

Cletus Brun surprised Fargo. He didn't get mad or angry. All he said was, "What makes you think so?"

"He made mention of a partner he was working with," Fargo revealed. "I think that partner was you."

"Because I'm a local like he was? I suppose I might think the same if I was in your boots. But you're barkin' up the wrong tree. I never partner up with anyone."

"So you claim."

Cletus rubbed his chin and said very deliberately, "You pile on the insults. Seems to me you're askin' for a poundin'

60

and I'm just the coon to oblige. Before this weekend is out I'm goin' to bust your bones."

"You're welcome to try."

"Here now," Tom said again. "I won't have talk like this, you hear me? Especially from you, Mr. Brun. I'm the one who hired you. To hunt for me, need I remind you? Not to indulge your violent tendencies."

"My what?" the block of muscle said, and laughed. "You and your fancy words. A man sticks up for himself and he's bein' violent? It's a good thing you're payin' me good money or I'd as soon pound you as him."

"Enough of this," Tom said. "Come with me." He reined around and his giant doppelganger went with him.

After that Fargo was left alone, which suited him as he had a lot to work out in his head. The way he saw it, he had at least three killers to contend with: the brown-eyed brother and sister, and whomever Anders had been working with. There was also the matter of who hired them. Since it was unlikely the same person hired both the brother and sister and the locals, that meant two of the four Clyborns were out to gain the inheritance at any cost. But which two? Charlotte was young and innocent. Samantha seemed genuinely to care for her siblings. Roland didn't seem the type. That left Tom, and Fargo wouldn't put anything past him.

The upshot, Fargo reflected, was that he better be more on his guard than ever.

Presently they came out of the trees into a clearing several acres in extent. Not a natural clearing, a man-made one where every oak and maple and pine had been felled to use as lumber in the construction of the Clyborn hunting lodge.

Fargo expected it to be big since the Clyborns never did anything on a small scale and he wasn't disappointed. The lodge covered two of the three acres. The logs had been precisely laid, the gaps chinked with Missouri clay. It looked sturdy enough to survive the apocalypse. At no doubt considerable expense, glass panes had been brought in and a custom door mounted. As at the mansion, there were a number of outbuildings, including a stable.

Samantha took charge, giving orders like a military commander. A small army of servants leaped to obey.

Not an hour after arriving, Fargo found himself in a spacious dining room at a long mahogany table, sipping piping hot coffee. Samantha had gone off to talk to the cook about supper. Tom had gone upstairs to unpack, taking Cletus Brun along. So had Charles with his friend from the club. Roland was outdoors. That left Charlotte and her cousin, Amanda, and Theodore Pickleman. The lawyer filled a china cup and sat next to the women.

"Well, my dears. At six this evening I will read the part of the will that explains the hunt, and who knows? It could be you, Charlotte, who inherits everything."

"I doubt that very much," Charlotte said. "I'm no hunter."

"If you are the one, I hope you will continue to retain me as the family attorney. I have always been faithful and done as was asked of me to the best of my ability."

"My father used to say you were a great help to him."

"A great man, your father." Pickleman raised his coffee cup in salute. "No one misses him more than I do."

Fargo thought the lawyer was laying it on a little thick but since the lawyer had brought it up, he asked, "What do you stand to gain out of all this?"

"I beg your pardon?"

"Are you in the will, too?"

"Would that I were," Pickleman said, and sighed. "Tom Senior never mixed business with his personal life. I knew him a good many years and he sometimes invited me to meals and had me over on holidays but I knew there was a line I didn't dare cross."

"He paid you well," Charlotte said.

"Yes, he did," Pickleman replied. "I can't complain in that respect."

Amanda excused herself to go to her room, saying she needed to rest after their long ride. She was a quiet girl, rather plain, and had a nice smile.

Shortly after, Pickleman drifted out, too.

No sooner did the lawyer leave than Charlotte stood and came down the table to a chair next to Fargo's.

"Were you serious, what you said?"

"About?" Fargo prompted.

"About wanting me."

About to drain his cup, Fargo peered at her over the rim. The Clyborns were a constant source of surprise. "I've never met a fine-looking woman I didn't want," he confessed. "Why?"

Charlotte sat very straight and stiff in her chair and said, "Because if you still do, I'd like very much for you to take me upstairs and ravish me."

9

The bedrooms were as lavish as everything else. Curtains on the windows, carpet on the floor, a four-poster bed with a canopy and a writing table and a chest of drawers.

Charlotte Clyborn had been wringing her hands on the climb up the stairs and now she walked to the window and parted the curtains and looked out. "It won't be supper for a couple of hours yet."

Fargo closed the door behind him and leaned against it, his arms across his chest. "Why did you really want to get me up here?"

Charlotte glanced over her slender shoulder and blinked those sweetly innocent eyes of hers. "Whatever do you mean?"

"It wasn't to ravish you," Fargo quoted her. Downstairs he had read fear in her face, and something else. She was as skittish as a colt in a lightning storm and he would like to learn why.

"What makes you so sure?"

"Quit playing games."

Charlotte tittered. "You think you know how I am but you don't. No one does except my cousin, Amanda. She and I have been close since the time I got to stay over at her house and we snuck her brother into our room." Charlotte tittered again. "My own brothers and sisters certainly don't know me. They think of me as this little darling who's never done any wrong."

Fargo didn't say anything. An uneasy feeling had come over him. The Clyborns were about to surprise him once again.

"Emmett was the real innocent. Our family was everything to him. Despite all that's happened he cared for each and every one of us. Even Tom. But now Emmett is dead and the innocence has died with him."

"You don't sound broken up about it."

Charlotte turned. A change had come over her. The sweet smile was gone, replaced by a cold smirk. "Why should I be? All Emmett was to me was another obstacle. Just as my sister is an obstacle."

"I don't savvy."

"Sure you do. You're not dumb. You just don't want to. You're like the rest. You think of me as pure and nice when I'm anything but."

Fargo had rarely misjudged anyone as badly as he had this snip of a well-endowed girl. "All this is leading up to something."

Charlotte came across the room and stood in front of him. "I'm being honest with you because I want you on my side and no one else's."

"Your sister hired me," Fargo reminded her.

"Why not work for her and for me, both?" Charlotte proposed. "I'd make it worth your while. Help me win the hunt and I'll give you ten times what she's offered you. Twenty thousand dollars. How does that sound?"

"Like a lot of money."

"Think of all the things you could spend it on. The poker games. The wenches. The drinking you could do."

Fargo had to smile. She had him pegged.

"That's not all I'm offering." Charlotte stepped so close that her bosom pressed his chest and her legs were against his. Her warm breath fanned his cheek. "I'm offering myself, as well. Ravish me. Do with me as you will. All I require is that you agree to side with me against Sam."

A cold feeling grew in the pit of Fargo's stomach, and spread. "It was all an act? In the clearing today?"

"My pretending to be shocked when you compared me to a ripe cherry?" Charlotte laughed. "Yes, I was having fun with you. I do that a lot. Have fun with people. Especially my family."

"Hell," Fargo said.

"What's the matter? You sound disappointed. Or are your feelings hurt, me playing you for a fool? Don't be offended. Be glad I've confided the truth. Be thrilled about the twenty thousand dollars. Most of all, be excited that I'm offering myself to you."

"Is that what you're doing?"

For an answer Charlotte pressed flush and raised her soft lips to his. The tip of her tongue rimmed his lips. When she drew back she made a clucking sound. "You can do better than that. The stories I've heard make you out to be the best lover who ever lived. Prove it. Show me you're worth baring myself to you."

The cold in Fargo changed to hot anger. He stared at her, and without any hint of what he was going to do, thrust his hand between her legs.

Charlotte gasped and threw her head back, her red lips parted in a "O" of surprise. "You get right to it, don't you?"

Fargo cupped a breast and squeezed hard through the fabric of her riding outfit. She moaned, and color crept up her face.

"Not so rough. That almost hurt."

"Did it?" Fargo said, and cupped her other mound. He squeezed just as hard and pulled her close, mashing his mouth against hers, delving his tongue into her mouth.

Cooing softly in her throat, Charlotte melted against him. Her hands rose and linked behind his neck. Her knee rose up and down. "Do me," she breathed into his ear.

Fargo had every intention. Bending, he swept her into his arms and carried her to the four-poster bed. He didn't set her down; he threw her onto her back hard enough to cause the canopy to shake.

"I'm not a sack of flour, you know."

Fargo got on the bed on his knees and pushed her legs apart and hitched at his belt.

"Hold on. I like to work up to it. Aren't we going to kiss and fondle some first?"

Taking her hand, Fargo placed it on his hardening manhood. "You need something to fondle, fondle this."

"Oh my." Charlotte's eyes widened and acquired a hungry cast. "You're a big one, aren't you?" She ran her palm up and down. "Goodness. No wonder the ladies like you so much."

Fargo kissed her to shut her up. He pried at her buttons and stays and soon had her jacket undone and her blouse opened, exposing her mounds. They were full and firm, her nipples like tacks. He pinched one and then the other and she squirmed under him.

"I said not to be so rough."

Fargo inhaled a nipple. He nipped it then bit it and he wasn't gentle, neither. She squirmed and sucked in her breath, then pushed on his chest and hiked her hand as if to slap him.

"Damn it. I won't tell you again. You're making me mad. Be gentle or get out."

Gripping her wrists, Fargo pinned them on the quilt. He kissed her lips, her throat, her ear. He bit the lobe and she stifled an outcry and tried to pull free.

"That was the last straw! Let go of me."

Fargo nuzzled her neck and roved the tip of his tongue over one breast and then the other.

"Didn't you hear me?"

Letting go of her left wrist, Fargo dipped his hand low over her skirt. She pushed against his shoulders, although not with much force. He looked at her and smiled. "You little bitch."

"What did you just call me?"

By then Fargo's hand was up and under. Her cotton drawers had a tie. A flick, and he was where he wanted to be. "I called you what you are," he said, and cupped her nether mound.

"Oh! Oh God."

Fargo parted her nether lips with the tip of his finger and rubbed her tiny knob, eliciting a moan. She dug her fingernails into his shoulders so deep it hurt.

"Like that, do you?" Fargo said, and lanced a finger up into her.

Charlotte arched up off the bed, then slowly sank back. She ground her hips to meet this thrusts and uttered tiny bleats of pleasure.

Fargo inserted a second finger. The bed was moving under them, the quilt bunching about their legs. With his other hand he undid his belt buckle and tugged at his pants.

"God, I love that. Don't stop."

Spreading her legs, Fargo positioned himself. In a deft move he slid his fingers out, aligned his pole, and impaled her to the hilt. He thrust deep and thrust hard, his knees rocking like steam engine pistons, his mouth on her throat and her breasts.

"Ah! Ah! Ah!" Charlotte cried out, and bit her lip. She gripped his sides and said, "Slower. Go slower."

Fargo did the opposite. He went faster, ramming into her again and again.

Breathing noisily through her nose, Charlotte raised her legs and locked her ankles behind his back.

"Damn you."

"Not much longer," Fargo said.

"No. Don't you dare. Let me first. If you do and peter out on me I might not."

Fargo almost said it would serve her right. Gripping her hips, he shut everything from his mind except the exquisite feel of her velvet tunnel. Usually he liked to take longer. Not

68

this time. She clawed and bucked and the next thing Fargo knew he was on the cusp. He shivered and shook and exploded.

His set off hers. Charlotte's mouth gaped wide and she levered up, and it was a wonder the canopy didn't crash down on their heads. "Yes! Yes! Oh, God, Yes!" She spurted and spurted.

Gradually Fargo slowed. He pulled out and eased onto his side with his head on his arm.

"Damn you to hell," Charlotte said.

"You're welcome."

"You did that on purpose. I wanted to take our time. We have the rest of the afternoon."

Fargo rolled onto his back and his hat came off. He put it back on, tugged his pants up, and buckled his belt.

"Say something, damn you."

"You should have been honest with me."

Charlotte rose on an elbow and poked him in the chest. "You're acting awful high and mighty. I had to keep up my act. Sam and the others think I'm a saint and they need to go on thinking that. It's the only advantage I have."

"You want the inheritance for yourself."

"What a stupid thing to say. Of course I do. Anyone with any brains would want the same. You don't think Sam wants it? Or Tom? Or Charles? They'd kill to get it, the same as me."

Fargo took note of that. "You didn't mention Roland."

"He's not as greedy as the rest of us. All he's ever cared about is being out in the woods hunting and whatnot."

Sitting up, Fargo swung his legs over the side of the bed. "See you around."

"Wait a minute." Charlotte grabbed at his buckskins. "Let's get a few things settled first. Now that you're working for me I want you to—"

"Sam," Fargo said.

"What?"

"Samantha hired me, not you." Fargo stood and adjusted his Colt so it rode on his hip.

"We have an agreement, you and I. Twenty thousand dollars, remember? More money than you've probably ever had in your entire life."

"I never said I'd take it."

Charlotte sat erect, her breasts jiggling with the movement. "Now, you just hold on. You never said you wouldn't, either. I took it for granted you accepted. Why else do you think I let you make love to me?"

Fargo cupped himself low down. "You did it for this." He smiled and made for the door. As he came around the foot of the bed she flew at him, growling like a wildcat. He caught her wrists as she went to rake his face and held firm. She kicked at his knee and he sidestepped. "Enough."

"You son of a bitch!" Charlotte was nearly beside herself. She drove a knee at his manhood and he twisted so his thigh took the blow. "No one does this to me. Do you hear me? No one."

Fargo pushed her onto the bed. She immediately began to get back up but he wagged a finger and said, "I wouldn't."

"Bastard."

"Bitch."

"You don't dare hurt me!" Charlotte hissed. "I'll have you arrested." Her face lit with vicious guile. "That's it! I'll tell everyone you raped me. I'll have you thrown behind bars so you can't take part in the hunt. All it will take is a scream loud enough to raise the roof." She opened her mouth wide.

"Go right ahead," Fargo said. "And while the sheriff is arresting me I'll tell him about the killers you hired."

Charlotte froze.

"You'll have to scream louder than that."

"What are you talking about?"

Fargo turned and walked to the bedroom door. She called his name and he paused with his hand on the latch.

"I did no such thing. You're making that up."

"Am I?" Fargo opened the door.

"You think you're clever but you're not. You trust Sam and you shouldn't. There's more to this than you can imagine. The truth is, you're a bumpkin in over his head and it's going to get you planted six feet under."

"And you're a money whore with her tits hanging out." Fargo shut the door and heard something thud against it. He grinned as he walked down the hall. He'd enjoyed that. But she was right about one thing: he *had* been only guessing about her hiring killers.

He could only hope she was wrong about that last part.

10

Samantha sat at one end of the long mahogany table, Tom at the other end. Fargo was on Sam's right, Cletus Brun on Tom's left. There were plenty of empty chairs; the table could seat forty people. Clockwise after Fargo, a few chairs away, sat Roland, then Theodore Pickleman. On the other side of the table were Charles and his friend from the Hannibal Men's Club, a man by the name of Bruce Harmon. Charlotte and her cousin Amanda sat across from Fargo and Charlotte glared at him every chance she got.

The meal started with a choice of soup, potato or vegetable. A salad bowl was passed around. Roast venison, beef and ham were the meats. Carrots and green beans the vegetables. In addition, the cook's staff had prepared simmering hot rolls. Fargo smeared his thick with butter. The coffee was a rich blend from Italy, he was told. The taste was too bitter for his liking so he spooned in enough sugar to sink a canoe. For dessert there was apple pie, cherry pie, or pudding. Fargo chose the pudding.

By six everyone was done eating and they were sitting around making small talk.

Fargo was on his fourth cup of coffee. No one said much to him, which was fine, as he got to eat in peace.

Then Samantha caught his eye. "I trust the meal was to your liking?"

"Kings should eat this well."

Sam grinned. "For all our father's faults, he was a stickler for family meals. We were required to eat together. No exceptions. Charles always had to wait to go to his club until after we ate. Roland stayed away more than a few times when he was off hunting, which always made Father furious."

Charlotte was being her sweet self around the others. She sighed and said with only slight resentment, "Our father always had to do everything his way. He never allowed for our personal wishes."

"Did you cry at his funeral?" Fargo asked.

"Why, of course I did," Charlotte answered, sounding shocked. "I loved my father even though he was always mean to me."

"Maybe he saw you for how you truly are."

Charlotte forgot herself and bristled. "What exactly is that supposed to mean? I was always the nicest of all of us."

"Emmett was nice, too," Samantha said sadly.

"Yes, he was," Charlotte quickly corrected herself. "I miss him terribly. It's a shame we can't give him a proper burial until after the hunt."

As if that were a cue, Theodore Pickleman rose and tapped his wineglass with a butter knife. The *ting-ting-ting* got everyone's attention. They all fell silent save for Tom, who loudly declared, "Finally!"

"We all know why we're here," the lawyer began. "It's yet another condition of your father's will. He was quite explicit in how this was to be arranged and I have followed his instructions to the letter."

"Yes, yes, get on with it," Tom said.

Charles leaned on his elbows. "How is this silly hunt to be handled?"

"I'll get to that in a moment." Pickleman hooked his thumbs in his vest. "First I am required to make one thing perfectly clear. Whoever wins the hunt inherits *everything*. All of your father's money. All of his many properties. All of his holdings in everything. We are talking millions of dollars."

"We know that," Tom said.

"Yes. But what you don't know is that in your father's will, he left it up to the winner to decide whether he or she will share any of the inheritance. Whoever prevails can either keep it all or offer the others equal shares."

"Equal?" Charlotte said.

Pickleman nodded. "It's a condition of the will. Either the winner shares everything equally or he or she can't share anything at all."

Roland said, "How peculiar."

"Not at all," Samantha said. "It's just like Father to force us to be generous whether we want to be or not. Don't you see? If Tom were to win, for instance, he can't keep ninety percent of the inheritance for himself and give the rest of us a pittance."

Tom took exception. "Why use me as your example? The rest of you would do the same."

"Perhaps. Perhaps not," Samantha responded. "A moot point since Father doesn't give us the choice."

"Even from the grave he controls our lives," Charles remarked.

"I can't wait for this to be over with," Charlotte said. "It's so morbid."

Theodore Pickleman cleared his throat. "May I get on with the details, please?" He paused. "The conditions are these. Tomorrow morning at six a.m. the hunt is to begin. You will have twenty-four hours in which to succeed. No more and no less. By six a.m. Monday morning, if none of you have claimed the prize, all of you forfeit any right to the inheritance."

Tom started to come out of his chair. "What the hell? You never said anything about this."

"I was required not to."

"Forfeit?" Charles repeated in stunned amazement. "Father would deny us everything?"

Samantha gestured to get the lawyer's attention. "What happens to the inheritance? Who gets it if we don't?"

"All your father's properties are to be sold off. All the

money from the proceeds and all the money in his bank accounts are to be administered to the poor and the needy."

Now Tom did come out of his chair. He was so incensed, he pounded the table. "We're to be deprived of what is rightfully ours to feed some dirt farmers? By God, I won't stand for this."

"The will is ironclad," Pickleman told him. "You can fight it in court but I can promise you that you'll lose."

"A bunch of poor riffraff," Tom said in disgust. "What have they done to earn it? Nothing."

Roland asked the question uppermost on Fargo's own mind. "What are we to hunt? All this talk of the inheritance and you still haven't said whether it's a bear or an elk or some other animal."

"Your father calls it a hunt in his will. Given what's at stake, and what you are to find, I'd call it a treasure hunt."

"Find?" Roland echoed. "We're not to track and kill game?"

"No. I'm afraid your hunting skills won't give you an edge. You see"—the lawyer gazed at each of them in turn—"the object of your hunt is a small wooden chest. In it is the last page of the will, bequeathing everything to whoever finds it."

"I'll be damned," Charles said.

"A treasure chest?" Tom swore lustily. "We're to decide our fate with some silly child's game?"

Pickleman answered, "Believe it or not, your father was trying to be fair. He buried the chest himself. I am permitted to tell you that it is within half a mile of the lodge, but in which direction, not even I know."

"That's a lot of ground to cover," Charlotte said.

"Which is why your father gave you twenty-four hours. He provided no other clues. There's no mention of landmarks or anything else that would help you. All I know is that he told me he had buried it in a shallow hole and that whoever found it would have no cause to weep."

"An understatement if ever I heard one," Tom spat. "And

so like our father. God, I hate him as much now as I did when he was alive." He glanced at Cletus Brun. "As for you, your hunting skills are of no use whatsoever."

"I can still be of help," the big Missourian said. "Four eyes are better than two and my eyes are sharp."

Samantha smiled ruefully at Fargo. "I had you come all this way thinking you were the best hunter my money could buy."

"You don't want me now?"

"To the contrary. Mr. Brun is right. Four eyes are better than one. Besides, it's too late to find someone else."

Pickleman tinged the glass again. "There are a few other conditions of which you must be aware. First, you must conduct the hunt on foot. No horses or mules allowed."

"Leave it to Father to make it as hard as possible," Charles said.

"Second, no weapons are allowed. No guns of any kind. No knives or anything else. All weapons are to be left here in the lodge."

Cletus Brun wasn't happy. "The hell you say! I never go anywhere unarmed. Only a fool does."

Fargo didn't like it, either. He would feel naked without his Colt or the Henry or the Arkansas toothpick. They were as much a part of him as his clothes, hat, and boots.

"The third condition is one I argued against," the attorney was saying. "I told your father that it is immoral and unethical. Inhuman might be a better word. He refused to rescind it."

"What is it?" Tom demanded.

Pickleman coughed. "Should any of you come to harm, no charges are to be lodged against whoever is responsible."

"What?" Samantha said.

The siblings sat there in silence as the full import slowly sank in. Finally Charles placed his hands on the table and cocked his head at the attorney. "Did we hear you correctly? Our father is encouraging us to attack one another?"

"That would be illegal," Pickleman said.

Tom was livid. "Don't try to hoodwink me. I'm no simpleton. What Father has done is set up a hunting contest where *we* are the game."

"He wouldn't," Samantha declared in horror. "Not even he would go that far."

"But he has," Charlotte said.

Cousin Amanda broke her long silence to say, "You're going to try and *kill* each another?"

"Only if we want to," Tom said, and laughed.

"There was no mention of anything like this," Amanda said. "I don't want any part of it."

"Nor do I," said Charles's friend, Bruce Harmon.

"That is entirely up to you," the lawyer told them. "In fact, the same applies to the principals." He looked at each of the siblings in turn. "Any of you can bow out if you so desire. Keep in mind that those who do are eliminated from the hunt and won't receive a cent of the inheritance."

"Our father," Roland said. "The devil in disguise."

Tom turned to Cletus Brun. "What about you? Are you as cowardly as our cousin and Bruce? Or will you see it through?"

"You're payin' me," Cletus replied.

"I'll take that as a yes."

Samantha focused on Fargo. "And you, Skye? Please think carefully before you answer. I don't want you to come to harm on my account."

Fargo fully realized the danger he was placing himself in as he said, "I gave my word I would take part." He turned. "But there's something all of you are overlooking."

"What would that be?" Pickleman said.

"Emmett. Whoever hired the man who shot him isn't done. Any one of you could be next."

"Which would please our deceased father no end," Tom said. "Or haven't you gotten it yet? He *wants* us to murder one another. He *wants* his own sons and daughters to kill one another off."

"Someone should report this to the sheriff," Amanda said.

Charlotte spun on her. "Don't you dare. This is a family matter and will be settled by us, not the law."

"You can settle it without bloodshed," Amanda persisted. "Each of you can give his or her word that you won't try to harm anyone else during the hunt."

"We could," Tom said, nodding, "but I won't."

"Why in God's name not?" Charles asked.

"Because I agree with Father. This is the best way. We've been at one another's throats for years. Fear of being thrown behind bars has always held us back but now we can give free rein to all the hate bubbling inside of us."

"You have a warped mind," Samantha said.

"As did Father." Tom chortled. "Ironic, is it not, that I'm more like him than any of you, yet I'm the one he thought was the fruit of someone else's loins?"

"So Charles and Charlotte will hunt by themselves?" Pickleman asked to have it clarified. "Amanda and Bruce have dropped out?"

Both their cousin and Harmon nodded.

"Just so you know," the lawyer told them, "you have until the actual start of the hunt to change your minds."

"I certainly won't," Bruce Harmon said.

Pickleman gazed along the table. "At six o'clock tomorrow morning I expect everyone to be out front. I am to fire a pistol to start the hunt. Remember, no mounts, no weapons, and no food or water."

Samantha straightened. "Father made that a condition, too? Twenty-four hours without anything to eat or drink smacks of cruelty."

"Our father's middle name," Tom said sarcastically.

Pickleman walked to the doorway. "I bid you good night. Since I am to oversee the hunt, I must remain awake the entire twenty-four hours. In order to do that I need all the sleep I can get tonight." He smiled and left.

"How can any of us sleep knowing what's in store?" Charlotte played her part as the innocent.

Fargo could use some rest himself. The lovemaking and the huge meal had left him sluggish and tired. He pushed back his chair and was about to excuse himself when Samantha placed her warm hand on his.

"Does all of this trouble you as much as it does me?" She didn't wait for him to reply. "We need to talk over our strategy for tomorrow."

"I'm listening."

"Not at the table. The others will overhear us. We need somewhere private." Samantha's cherry lips curled and her fingernail traced a delicate line across this hand. "Why don't you come up to my room with me?"

Oh hell, Fargo thought.

11

Samantha Clyborn was as attractive a female as Skye Fargo ever met. Her gorgeous hair, her piercing eyes, her hourglass figure were enough to make any male drool. But Fargo was tired and feeling sluggish from the big meal. He'd also bedded her sister not more than two hours ago. As he followed Sam's sashaying form down the hall to her bedroom, he hoped to God his body could rise to the occasion.

Samantha paused at the door. "Thank you for waiting at the table a couple of minutes before you got up and followed me. I didn't want my sister and brothers to suspect."

Fargo looked at her bosom and at the swell of her hips, and nodded.

"Not that there's anything wrong with me inviting a man up to my room," Sam quickly added. She opened the door and motioned for him to enter but Fargo shook his head and gestured for her to go first.

Her bedroom smelled of lavender. Thick purple carpet covered the floor. Her bed was bigger than Charlotte's and covered with a purple quilt. The fringed canopy was purple, too.

"Your favorite color?"

Sam had stepped to a full-length mirror and was fluffing her air. "What? Oh, yes. I've liked it ever since I was little and learned it's the color of royalty. I always thought that fitting."

Fargo didn't savvy and said so.

"I should think it obvious." Sam smoothed her dress, then

faced him. "In Britain and Europe the ruling class is royalty. Kings, queens, dukes, princes and the like. Over here the ruling class is the class with money. The class my family belongs to. We hold all the power. We control the conditions under which those who don't have money live."

"You think of yourself as royalty?"

"In a way, yes." Sam went to the bed and ran a hand over the purple quilt. "Don't get me wrong. I don't think I'm better than those who don't have any. Quite the contrary. I see it as a great responsibility. Although"—she stopped and bit her lip— "it's a moot point since by Monday morning I won't have any money or any power if I lose the hunt."

"I'll do my best."

"I have no doubt you will." Samantha turned and walked up to him, her hips swaying, her hands clasped to her bosom. "But I didn't really invite you up here to talk strategy."

"You said you did."

"I lied." Sam placed a hand on his chest and bored her eyes into his. Her voice grew husky as she asked, "Do you have any idea how long it has been since I've been with a man?"

"How would I?"

"Let's just say I rarely permit myself the luxury. But I'll confess something to you." Her breath warmed his neck as she quietly said, "I've wanted you from the moment I laid eyes on you."

"Do tell."

"There's something about you." Sam touched his chin. "It's not just that you're so damn handsome. There's something else, some quality I can't describe."

"Don't get carried away."

"I'm serious." A puzzled look came over her as she traced a finger from his beard to his cheek and over to his ear. "I've puzzled over it no end and I can't explain why I feel the way I do. I've met other men just as handsome who didn't affect me the way you do."

"Lucky me."

"Please. I'm being serious and you're being sarcastic." Sam pursed her strawberry lips. "When a lady compliments a man the least the man can do is accept the compliment graciously."

"My manners aren't what they should be," Fargo enlightened her. "And I don't give a damn that they're not."

"Ah. The rough-hewn frontiersman. You don't care for society or its rules. Is that how it goes?"

"I don't much care for buffalo shit no matter what others call it."

Samantha drew back. "I beg your pardon?"

"All the airs that you and those like you put on don't count for a hill of beans. Nothing you do will live on after you. You've spent your whole life thinking you're special because your family has money, but in the end you land in the ground like all those who don't have any."

"All is vanity, yes." Samantha looked him up and down. "Frankly, I didn't expect that of you."

"I'm too dumb to think?"

"No, no, it's not that."

Fargo noticed that she didn't offer a better reason. "I'll make it plain. I like you but I don't like your airs."

Sam's face colored and she fingered a button on her dress. "And I don't like how you talk to me sometimes. But please. Let's forget all that. We can't help how we are. I didn't ask for this life of privilege."

"But you sure eat it up."

Samantha turned her back to him. "This isn't how it was supposed to go. I had other things in mind."

Fargo saw her reflection in the mirror; she looked sad. Walking up behind her, he molded his body to hers, reached around, and cupped her mounds.

Sam gasped and arched her back. "What do you think you're doing?"

"What you invited me up here to do." Fargo squeezed and was rewarded with a soft groan and the grinding of her bottom against his manhood. He felt himself twitch, and smiled.

"I thought maybe you wouldn't want to."

"Airs or not, you're female." Fargo bent and kissed her neck and she twisted half around and cupped his chin.

"Is that all I am to you? You don't care for me even a little bit?"

"I told you I like you. It's not true love, if that's what you're thinking."

"It's just that a woman likes to think she means something."

Fargo could have told her that the hunger she stirred in him was no different from the hunger that stirred him to eat or the thirst that stirred him to drink. He could have said that she was putting on yet another air. But he didn't. He said, "Every woman means something in bed."

Sam blinked and cocked her head. "I don't know whether to be flattered or insulted."

"You'll talk it to death if you're not careful." Fargo drew back. "Make up your mind."

"I want to. I really do."

"Then shut the hell up." Fargo kissed her, hard, and thrust his tongue into her mouth. With his one hand he squeezed a breast while with his other he caressed her thighs and cupped her mound of Venus. Another moan escaped her, and she sucked on his tongue as if it were honey.

Pushing her back, Fargo eased her onto the bed. Her hair spilled about her head as she looked up at him in raw lust.

"God, I want you."

"Don't talk." Fargo covered her mouth with his and sank down beside her. He ran his hands over her body, probing, massaging, stroking. She took off his hat and ran her fingers through his hair, then worked at his belt buckle.

Fargo reached down, took her hand, and placed it on his pole. She uttered a tiny mew and melted against him, her fingers wrapped around his member.

"Oh my," she breathed.

Fargo began undoing the dress. A row of tiny buttons that ran from the nape of her neck to the small of her back took forever. He would as soon have ripped the dress off her. At last he slipped a hand underneath. A few tugs at the tie to her drawers and his hand brushed silken thighs. She squirmed as he kneaded them. Inching higher, he covered her nether lips.

"Yes! Ohhhh, yes!"

Fargo plunged a finger in. Her mouth became molten; she kissed and licked and sucked with abandon. A few moments more and he had her breasts free. Her nipples poked into his palms like tacks.

Samantha raked his shoulders with her nails and pushed against him. Her legs parted in invitation.

Fargo was so intent on their lovemaking that he almost didn't hear the rasp of the latch. He was sucking on a nipple, and glanced over.

A young maid had entered and was staring at them. She wore the usual purple uniform and was holding a silver tray with a pitcher of water.

Fargo figured she would make a hasty exit but she stared at him with her lips curled in a strange sort of grin. He raised his head from Sam's melons.

"What's the matter? Why have you stopped?"

"We have company."

Samantha twisted around. "What the hell? I gave instructions I wasn't to be disturbed."

Without looking behind her, the maid pushed the door shut with her foot.

"What in God's name do you think you're doing?" Samantha angrily demanded.

The maid threw the bolt.

"Are you insane? Leave this moment or you're no longer in my employ."

There was something about the maid's face that triggered sudden alarm in Fargo. She had her hair up in a bun and it took him a few seconds to realize where he had seen her before—it was the female assassin who had tried to kill him on the *Yancy* and helped her brother slay Tobacco Man. He pulled at his pants and started to roll off the bed, his member jutting like a flagpole.

"What are you doing?" Sam asked.

The maid exploded into motion. In two bounds she was at the bed. She had hold of the pitcher and before Fargo could duck or dodge she swept it up and out. The water caught him full in the face, getting into his eyes and his nose. Blinking and backpedaling, Fargo swiped a sleeve across his eyes to clear his vision.

The pitcher and the tray hit the floor with a crash. The maid's hands flashed behind her and flashed out again, each holding a knife. She slashed at Samantha, who recoiled, and then she was around the bed in a crouch, still grinning her strange grin, her eyes alight with glee.

Fargo stabbed for his Colt but it wasn't there. His gun belt was lying on the bed.

The holy terror in the maid's uniform never said a word. She was all business, and her business was slaying him. Her knives weaved figure eights in the air.

"My pistol!" Fargo shouted to Sam but she was frozen in shock. He avoided a stab at his belly and a slash at his neck. He had to let go of his pants and they began to slide down his hips. Grabbing hold, he shifted to the right but went left. The feint saved his life.

The assassin lost her grin. She speared a knife at his chest and when he jerked aside lanced her other knife at his jugular.

Fargo flung himself back and collided with the wall. Inadvertently he had backed himself into a corner. He held on to his pants to keep them from falling and tried to spring past her but she was much too quick. He had to jerk back again to avoid having his throat cut from ear to ear.

"No!" Sam cried, and threw a pillow.

The assassin swatted it aside and came at Fargo again. He tried to grab her wrist and pain seared his upper arm. She had cut through the buckskin sleeve and drawn blood. Before she could skip out of reach he whipped a backhand that sent her staggering. Then, dropping to one knee, he plunged his hand into his boot and palmed the Arkansas toothpick. "Try me now, bitch."

In she rushed, her knives streaking.

Fargo parried, countered, parried again. He unfurled, moving back as he rose, and nearly tripped over his pants. He had forgotten to hold them up and they were bunching around his legs. Clutching them, he barely deflected a cut at his eyes. She was skilled, this woman, perhaps the best knife fighter he ever went up against, and that was saying a lot.

"I'll stop her!" Sam cried, and lunged for the Colt.

Once again the sister did her imitation of a jackrabbit. Whirling, she vaulted high in the air. Her foot slammed against Sam's head, knocking Sam back. As lithely as a cat, she alighted on the balls of her feet poised to renew their combat.

Fargo had never encountered her like. He slashed at her legs, at her ribs, but it was like trying to cut a will-o'-the-wisp.

She grinned her strange grin again. She held the right blade out from her side, the left blade low in front of her.

Fargo went for her face but she hopped out of reach. Her knives flashed and his middle knuckle was opened. Not deep but it hurt like hell. He went high, going for her throat, only to have her prance out of reach.

A revolver boomed. Sam had his Colt and fired from a distance of only a few feet—and missed.

The assassin spun. She leaped onto the edge of the bed and did an acrobatic somersault. Her right leg described an arc and her shoe caught Samantha on the chin and sent Sam tumbling.

Fargo sought to bury the toothpick in her back. So what if she was a woman? She had tried several times now to kill him and that was several too many. But as fast as he was she proved faster. She was halfway to the door before he came around the end of the bed. She worked the latch and threw the door wide, then paused in the doorway to look back.

"My compliments," she said.

Wondering what the hell she meant, Fargo dashed after her. It took barely two seconds for him to reached the doorway— yet the hallway was empty. He stood there with his arm stinging and his hand hurt and blood trickling from under his sleeve and summed up his sentiments with, "I'll be damned."

12

A search of the lodge from top to bottom turned up a discarded maid's uniform in a pantry but there was no trace of the deadly woman who wore it. Samantha was furious. She ordered that the lodge be searched again. When Charles remarked that the servants had already gone over every square foot and another search was pointless, Samantha blistered his ears. Charles proved to be right, though: the assassin had disappeared.

Samantha called a family meeting in the dining room. She insisted that her brothers and her sister attend, along with their partners in the hunt. Theodore Pickleman eased into a chair across from Fargo.

"All of you have heard what happened," Sam began. "My partner in the hunt tomorrow has been marked for murder. I'd like to know which of you is to blame for the attempts on his life."

"How dare you blame one of us," Tom indignantly replied.

"Who else?" Sam said. "The only people with anything to gain are sitting at this table."

"Why have they only tried to kill your partner?" Roland wondered. "I know the forest better than he does and no attempt has been made on my life. For that matter, Cletus Brun has lived in these woods since he was born yet no one has tried to kill him, either."

"Indeed," Charlotte said. "What makes Fargo so special?"

Fargo had been asking himself the same thing. "Maybe it's not me so much as your sister."

"How's that?" Samantha asked.

"It's you they want to stop," Fargo guessed. But why her more than any of the others was a mystery.

"You're forgetting Emmett," Roland said. "His death makes no sense at all."

"Maybe it does," Charles said, and glanced about sheepishly. "You see, there's something I haven't told any of you. Something that could explain why poor Emmett was shot."

"We're listening," Sam said.

Charles cleared his throat. "Emmett confided in me that he might have seen Father bury the chest."

The siblings all started talking at once. Tom pounded the table and demanded to know why Charles hadn't said anything sooner.

"Because Emmett asked me to keep it secret," Charles replied. "We were always close, the two of us, probably because we were born less than a year apart. The night before he was shot, he took me aside and told me that he had come out to the lodge one day to hunt grouse with Roland and saw Father go off through the woods carrying a shovel and a sack. Emmett was curious and followed him."

"Dear God," Charlotte said. "Emmett could easily have won."

"Except he didn't know what it was at the time," Charles said, "and he couldn't remember where he saw father bury the thing. He didn't pay much attention and got out of there quickly, afraid Father would spot him."

"Who else did Emmett tell?" Tom asked.

"No one, so far as I know."

"Someone must have overheard," Roland speculated. "But if that was the case, they had to know how important the chest is. And none of us knew that until this evening."

Tom was glaring at Charles. "It took you long enough to enlighten us."

"What are you implying?" Charles responded.

"Only that it's strange you didn't mention this earlier when Pickleman told us about the will."

Charles came out of his chair. "I don't like what you are implying. I loved Emmett as much as any of you. I would never harm him. As for wanting the inheritance, which of us doesn't?"

Fargo had heard enough bickering to last a lifetime. Pushing his chair back, he made for the door. Samantha called to him but he shook his head. He didn't stop until he was outside.

The sun was about to relinguish its reign. Vivid streaks of red, orange, and yellow splashed the western sky. Songbirds were in full throat and somewhere off in the trees a dove cooed.

Fargo strolled over to the stable. He checked on the Ovaro and was coming back out when a shadow fell across the center aisle, and him. Instinctively, he swooped his hand to his Colt.

"Hold on there, hoss. I'm friendly. Don't shoot."

"Show yourself."

Cletus Brun stepped into view. He was cradling his rifle, and nodded in a friendly fashion.

"What the hell do you want?"

The big Missourian frowned. "I can't say I care to be talked to that way."

"I can't say I care."

"You don't want to rile me. The last gent who did is crippled."

"Who hired Anders and you?"

"I told you before I didn't know Anders," Brun said. "What will it take to get that though your head?"

"Bucklin Anders and you were working together. He shot Emmett. Someone else hired two other killers and they killed Bucklin Anders." Fargo lowered his hand close to his Colt.

"Who hired you?"

"Where do you get these harebrained notions?"

"I figured out most of it," Fargo said. It wasn't hard. Anders had mentioned having a partner and Anders was a local. It stood to reason his partner was the same.

"You figured wrong. I wasn't in cahoots with him."

"Who hired you?"

"Are your ears plugged with wax?" Brun growled. "I've warned you and you refuse to listen. Don't ask me that again, you hear?"

"Who hired you?"

"You are a hardheaded son of a bitch." Brun started to turn and suddenly whipped around, swinging his rifle like a club.

Fargo was ready. He ducked and drew but as he cleared leather Brun's foot slammed his wrist and the Colt was jarred from his grasp. He lunged for it but Brun's rifle caught him on the shoulder, spinning him half around. He expected Brun to swing again and sidestepped, only to have a pair of arms twice the size of his own encircle his chest from behind.

"I've got you now, little man."

Fargo struggled mightily as Brun lifted him off the ground and shook him as a bear might shake a hound. Fargo's hat fell off. He tried to surge free but Brun's arms were bands of iron.

"I warned you not to rile me."

The pressure on Fargo's chest grew worse. The stable swam. He'd swear his ribs were about to stave in. In desperation he drove the back of his head against the Missourian's face. There was a *crunch* and a spurt of wet on his neck.

"Damn your hide!" Brun roared. "You've done busted my nose!"

Fargo rammed his head back again. Brun howled and spun and Fargo was sent stumbling. He smashed against a stall and sprawled onto his side, dazed. A black boot hooked down and agony lanced his ribs. Another blow flipped him onto his back. Struggling to stay conscious, he saw the boot rise over his face.

"I'm goin' to stomp you to a pulp."

Fargo drove his own boot up and in and caught Brun where it would hurt a man the most. The hulking slab of gristle and sinew cried out and stumbled, his hands over his groin.

Fargo made it to his hands and knees. He shook his head to clear it, saw Brun's legs, and slammed into them. His intent was to bowl Brun over and in that he succeeded. What he hadn't counted on was Brun falling on top of him.

Fargo was pinned. He sought to heave Brun off but it was like trying to heave an anvil. Brun growled and raised his big hands and wrapped them around Fargo's throat.

"If I can't stomp you I'll strangle you."

Fargo gripped Brun's wrists and pushed but couldn't budge them. He butted Brun in the face but all Brun did was grin and keep squeezing. Fargo's breath was cut off. He sucked air into his nose but it did no good. He was on the verge of plunging into a black well when he did the only thing he could think of to do: he dug his thumbs into Brun's eyes.

The Missourian howled. The pressure on Fargo's throat slackened but not enough; Fargo gouged his thumbs deeper. Suddenly Brun had hold of his wrists and Fargo was jerked to his feet. He could breathe and he could see again. Blood was trickling from both of Brun's eyes. Pits of hell, those eyes—filled with unbridled rage and undiluted hate.

"God *damn* you!"

A knee as big as a sledge smashed Fargo in the sternum. He was hurled against the wall and fell into some straw. Groping to get his hands under him, he felt something hard under his right hand. The shape took a few seconds to register. He gripped it just as Brun gripped him by the shoulders and spun him around. Brun cocked a huge fist. "It ends now."

"You've got that right." Fargo swung the horseshoe. Metal *thwucked* on flesh and Brun staggered. Fargo hit him again, and a third time.

"Don't," Brun said. He was swaying. Scarlet oozed from his split temple as he held out a hand. "I've had enough."

"You started it." Fargo hit him so hard it hurt his own hand. The crash of Brun striking the ground sent a tingle down Fargo's spine. He raised the horseshoe to strike once more but lowered his arm. He never could beat on someone once they were down.

Fargo cast the horseshoe aside and wiped his sleeve across his sweaty brow. He shuffled from the stable. Every muscle was sore. He was battered and bruised but he would live.

He hadn't learned much. He still didn't know which of the Clyborns had hired Brun and Anders. He still didn't know which of them had hired the brother and sister. He suspected Tom guilty of the former, possibly Charlotte of the latter. But it could be any of them.

A pair of servants in purple walked by and gave him odd looks. One of them asked, "Are you all right, sir? If you don't mind my saying, you look positively dreadful"

Fargo supposed he did. "Fine, thanks," he said, and shuffled on, gaining strength as he went. When he reached the lodge he went straight to his room. He made sure to throw the bolt and as an added precaution propped the chair against the door.

Fargo stood in front of the mirror. He did look awful. He threw his hat on the bed and stripped off his buckskin shirt. His chest and arms were a welter of black-and-blue marks. He filled the basin with water from the pitcher and washed the grime from his face and the dirt from his hair.

Weariness seeped in. It had been a long, eventful day. It was early yet but he stretched out on the bed on his back with the Colt in his hand, and closed his eyes. He tried to sleep but his mind wouldn't shut down. He reviewed all that had happened since he arrived. One fact was plainer than ever. He couldn't trust any of them. The Clyborns, Cletus Brun, the brother and sister assassins—any of them might try to do him in.

It promised to be an interesting hunt.

Fargo placed his forearm over his eyes. He yawned and

willed himself to relax. It hit him that he was under no obligation to stay. He could leave if he wanted. Take a day's pay and forget the rest. His life was worth more than two thousand dollars. To him, at least.

He mulled it over and decided that no, he couldn't go. He owed it to himself to see the hunt through. Too much had happened. He took it personal, the attempts on his life, and Brun trying to beat him senseless. He had never been one to turn the other cheek and he would be damned if he would start now.

Fargo started to drift off. A sound brought him out of himself, the faint scrape of the latch being tried. He opened his eyes. The latch was moving, but slowly. He swung his legs to the floor and crept to the door. He put his ear to it but couldn't hear anything. As quietly as possible he moved the chair. He eased the bolt, gripped the latch, and flung the door wide.

No one was there.

Fargo stepped out and looked right and left. The hallway was empty. He wondered if it could have been his imagination, but no, he had seen the latch move.

Someone had tried to enter.

Backing into the room, he secured the latch and once again propped the chair against it. He also took the pitcher and placed it next to the chair's leg so that if someone forced the door the racket would wake him from even the deepest sleep.

Voices from outside drew Fargo to the window. Tom and Charles were under a maple, arguing. Tom looked fit to punch his brother and was shaking his fist in Charles's face. As Fargo looked on, Charles wheeled and walked away.

What a family, Fargo thought. He laid back down. He must be a glutton for punishment, he told himself, to go through all this when he didn't have to.

Fargo recollected hearing that pride went before a fall. Maybe so, but he couldn't look at himself in the mirror if he quit.

One thing was certain. The two people who had died so far wouldn't be the only ones. There wasn't a shred of doubt in his mind that before the hunt was over more would be bucked out in gore.

Just so he wasn't one of them.

13

Fargo was up early. He splashed water on his face and shrugged into his shirt, wincing from the bruises. Shoving his hat on his head, he went to strap on his gun belt, and remembered—no weapons were allowed. Reluctantly, he left the Colt on the bed. He left the Arkansas toothpick in its ankle sheath. No one knew he had it and he might need it before the twenty-four hours were up.

Fargo thought he would be the first outside but he was mistaken. Too much was at stake. They were all there, waiting for the shot that would start the hunt.

Tom and Cletus Brun were at the bottom of the steps and glared at him when he stepped into the rosy light of the chill dawn. Charlotte was nervously pacing, her cousin at her side. Apparently Amanda had changed her mind about taking part. Charles stood alone, wrapped in his thoughts. Roland was gazing over the woodland.

Samantha wore a coat. She greeted him with, "Good morning, Skye. I hope you slept well."

"I wish."

Sam looked around as if to be sure she wouldn't be overheard and said, "It's a shame we were interrupted yesterday. After this is over maybe we can take up where we left off."

"Fargo was studying Cletus Brun. The big backwoodsman wasn't wearing a revolver or a knife—that Fargo could see.

But Brun's clothes were loose and bulky and could easily conceal a weapon.

Sam stared in the direction Fargo was looking. "I heard about the fight. A servant found Mr. Brun lying in the stable. He refused to say what happened but we've all guessed. Tom was furious. He told Pickleman that you shouldn't be allowed to take part in the hunt but Theodore said you hadn't broken any of the rules."

At that moment the lawyer emerged. He stifled a yawn, then said cheerfully, "Good morning. Is everyone ready for the day's excitement?" He grinned, but no one else did. "Yes, well." He consulted a pocket watch. "The hunt begins promptly at six. Another ten minutes yet."

"Why not start it now?" Tom said. "We're all here."

"Your father stipulated six o'clock and six it will be. The conditions in the will must be met."

"Leave it to you to be a stickler for Father's nonsense."

Pickleman tsked-tsked. "Really now. You can't fault me for going by the letter of the law."

"This whole thing is a farce," Charles said. "Father has set it up so that we're pitted against one another like roosters in a cockfight or dogs in a pit. He hated us so much, he wants to tear us apart from the grave."

"It's despicable," Samantha said.

Pickleman sniffed and declared, "Whether anyone is harmed is entirely up to all of you. Conduct the hunt fairly or be underhanded and mean. It's your choice."

"Too much is at stake to be fair," Tom said. "This isn't an inheritance hunt. It's a death hunt."

Sam stepped forward and raised her arms to get their attention. "I want everyone to know that I don't intend to fall for Father's ruse. I refuse to harm any of you."

Tom laughed. "You expect us to believe that?"

"Why wouldn't you? I've always treated every one of you with the utmost respect. You know that, Thomas."

"I know that with millions of dollars at stake I'd be a fool to trust you or any of the others. Siblings or not, it's every man, or woman, for him- or herself, and the devil take the hindmost."

"Exactly the attitude Father wanted to provoke."

Tom smirked. "Then he's succeeded. Make no mistake, dear sister. I want to win. I want the inheritance. If I lose, I lose everything. I'll be left with the clothes on my back and nothing more. I can't have that."

"Nor I," Charles said. "But I refuse to conduct the hunt like some animal. I won't harm any of you if you don't try to harm me."

Sam smiled and nodded. "That's two of us. How about you, Charlotte? Roland?"

Roland answered first. "I intend to keep to myself and expect the rest of you to do the same. Should I run into you in the woods I won't lift a finger against you unless you lift one against me."

Charlotte stopped her pacing. "I'd like to believe that none of us will hurt one another but Tom is right. Too much is at stake." She looked at her brothers and her sister. "It's not just that I *want* to win. I *need* to win. I need to find that damn chest because I refuse to be poor. I refuse to live like the common people do. I was born into luxury and I am going to go on living in luxury, the rest of you be damned."

"Thank you for being honest with us," Charles said dryly.

"Spare me your sarcasm," Charlotte shot back. "You're the same as me, what with your expensive men's club and your expensive clothes and your expensive food and drink. You need to win as much as I do."

"True," Charles conceded. "But I refuse to stoop to Father's level and resort to violence to do it."

"Sweetness and love. Isn't it glorious?" Tom laughed his brother to scorn. "All this is well and good but you're forgetting a few things, dear brother, as Fargo pointed out yesterday. You're forgetting Emmett, murdered by a killer who must have been hired by one of us. You're forgetting that other pair of assassins who are undoubtedly out there somewhere right this minute, waiting to do us in."

"I certainly didn't hire them," Samantha said.

"So you claim," Tom rejoined. "But how can we be sure? Charles and Roland have both said they will play nice but how do we know one or both of them hasn't paid to have the rest of us killed?"

"The same applies to you," Charles said.

"That it does," Tom agreed. "So it won't do me any good to give you my word that the assassins aren't my doing."

"As if we would believe you anyway," Charlotte said.

A strained silence fell, broken only when Sam turned to Theodore Pickleman. "I have a question about the hunt."

"Anything I can answer, I will," the lawyer assured her.

"Father said the chest is buried within half a mile of the lodge. Is that correct?"

"It is," Pickleman verified.

"I'm not much good at judging distances. How will I know when I've gone half a mile? I could end up going farther and waste a lot of time I could put to better use."

"Ah," Pickleman said. "I forgot to tell you, didn't I?"

"Tell us what?"

"Your father, as usual, thought of everything. Since he couldn't very well have a fence built to mark the boundary, he stipulated the next best thing. Yesterday, servants rode out half a mile in every direction and marked trees and boulders and logs with red paint. Spot those and you'll know to turn around."

Charles said, "You can't have marked every tree and boulder. We could easily miss them."

"True," Pickleman said. "As an added precaution, servants have been stationed at various points along the perimeter and will yell to any of you they see going past the half-mile mark."

Charles gave a sudden start and blurted, "I'll be damned."

"What?" Pickleman asked.

"Nothing," Charles said. "I was thinking of poor Emmett, is all."

The lawyer consulted his pocket watch. "Five minutes. Any of you who want a last drink or bite to eat should get it quickly."

No one moved.

"Very well. Remember, the hunt is to last twenty-four hours. Not a minute longer. If none of you have found the chest by six o'clock tomorrow morning, I'm to fire another shot and that will be the end of it."

"What if we keep looking and find the chest five minutes after six?" Charles asked.

"It doesn't matter. Six is the deadline. After that, the money and the holdings are to be administered by the executor and there is nothing you can do to stop it."

"One of us will find the damn thing long before that," Tom predicted.

"That could very well be," Pickleman said. "In which case I will fire four shots in the air, one after the other, to signal to the rest that the chest has been discovered."

Roland stepped up to Samantha and held out his hand. "I wish you luck, sister."

Sam looked at his hand and then at his face. She shook. "The same to you. Be careful out there."

"Watch out for snakes and bears," Roland cautioned. "Although with Fargo to help you, you should do fine."

"How touching," Tom said.

Roland turned. "I don't blame you for being cynical. But I want you to know something. I want all of you to know that if I find the chest, I'm sharing the inheritance. Each and every one of you will get an equal amount, both in money and in property."

"Always the noble one," Samantha said.

Tom chortled. "Oh, please. Next you'll have him walking on water."

"Must you be so cruel?"

"Must you be so gullible? Our dear brother says he will share now, but who can predict what he'll say if he's the one who finds the damn chest? He might change his mind."

"I wouldn't do that," Roland said.

"No, not someone so *noble*," Tom mocked him.

Her jaw twitching, Samantha went down the steps two at a stride, her dress swishing noisily.

Tom saw her coming. "Yes, dear sister? What's on your mind?"

Sam smacked him. She hit him so hard, she rocked Tom on his heels. Shocked, he put a hand to his cheek. Cletus Brun swore and started to reach for her but Tom swatted his hand away.

"Don't you dare. She might be a fool and she might be deluded but she's still my sister."

Sam had her arm poised to slap him again. "I won't have you talk like that to Roland. Do you hear?"

"Whatever you say," Tom said sullenly.

Theodore Pickleman announced, "Three minutes." Then he reached under his jacket and produced a pistol.

Fargo had been watching Samantha and didn't realize Charlotte was next to him until she touched his elbow.

"Have you thought over what we talked about?"

"I told you. I'm working for your sister."

"You can work for both of us. She doesn't have to know. If you find the chest, inform me, not her. You'll leave here with enough money to keep you in whiskey and whores for a year."

"A bottle a night adds up," Fargo said.

Charlotte gripped his wrist. "I'm serious."

"I already gave you my answer." Fargo pulled loose. "And if I see those two killers you hired, gun or no gun, it will be them or me."

"I didn't hire anyone, damn you. Certainly not that oafish Anders and not the brother and sister you say are trying to kill us."

Fargo almost believed her, she sounded so sincere. "If you're telling the truth you'd better keep one eye behind you or whoever did hire them will get to gloat over your corpse."

Charlotte gazed at her siblings and said fiercely, "It's turned out exactly as Father wanted. Here we are, at one another's throats, with no one believing a word anyone else says. He truly was a devil."

"Stay with your cousin at all times," Fargo advised. "Don't separate for any reason."

"What's this? Concern for my safety? When you just branded me a liar?"

"I could be wrong."

"You're a fool like all the rest," Charlotte said in disgust, and walked back to where Amanda was waiting.

"Two minutes," Pickleman said.

"I feel like a racehorse at the starting gate," Charles observed.

Fargo went down the steps to Samantha. She had moved away from the others and stood with her head bowed. "Are you all right?"

"I shouldn't have done that, lost my temper the way I did. Smacking him was wrong."

"He's a jackass."

"True," Sam agreed. "But he's also my brother and I care for him whether he believes I do or not." She sadly shook her head. "Father must be laughing in his grave."

"Maybe it will turn out all right."

"Listen to yourself. You know it won't. I have the feeling I'm setting eyes on some of them for the last time." Sam groaned. "If only we could call it off."

"One minute," the attorney hollered.

"I'll do what I can to protect you," Fargo promised. Not that there was a whole hell of a lot he could do when all he had was a knife.

"If it comes to that, protect the others, too. I'll pay you extra. I never expected anything like this when I sent for you."

"It's not the money," Fargo said.

"It is to us."

Theodore Pickleman pointed the pocket pistol at the sky and thumbed back the hammer. "The time has come, ladies and gentlemen. Let the inheritance hunt commence."

The shot was like the crack of doom.

14

The Missouri woods were thick and lush, the dense tangle of undergrowth nearly always in shadow. Fargo glided through it as silently as an Apache. He couldn't say the same about Samantha Clyborn.

Sam had bolted for the woods the instant the pistol went off. Charlotte had done the same, in a different direction, Amanda at her heels. Tom hurried into the trees to the north, urging Cletus Brun to go faster. Charles jogged to the south. Only Roland walked.

Fargo called out to Samantha to wait for him but she didn't listen. He ran to catch up and did so only after she stopped to get her bearings. "You're fast on your feet," he complimented her.

"I was a bit of a tomboy when I was little." Sam cast about, her face twisted in puzzlement. "Which way, do you think?"

Fargo shrugged. "One is as good as another."

"You're a big help." Samantha walked in a small circle, scratching her head. "There's so much ground to cover, I don't know where to begin."

"I didn't know your father. You did. Try to think like him," Fargo suggested. "Where would you bury the chest if you had done it?"

"Impossible to say," Samantha said. "No one thought like he did. That's why I sent for you. You're supposed to be the great frontiersman. How would you go about finding something if this were the mountains or the prairie?"

Fargo pondered. To the east the ground was mostly flat woodland. To the north and west were hills. To the south a creek ran close to the hunting lodge. Landmarks were few. The terrain was essentially the same—forest and more forest.

Sam impatiently tapped her foot. "I'm waiting for an idea."

"I don't have one."

Shaking her head in annoyance, Sam said, "I repeat. You're a big help. There must be something we can look for."

"A mound of dirt where your father buried it," was the only thing Fargo could come up with at the moment.

"All the chest contains is a page from the will so it need not be that big. Still, a pile of dirt should stand out."

"Unless it's under a bush."

They began the search in earnest. Samantha suggested they separate to cover more ground and Fargo reminded her of the assassins.

"Damn them to hell, anyway. Whoever hired them should be hung."

Fargo put his hand on his hip where his Colt would ordinarily be, and frowned. He didn't like not having a gun. He didn't like it at all. He was about to bend and draw the toothpick from the ankle sheath and slide it under his belt when the undergrowth behind them crackled. He whirled just as the last person he expected stepped toward them.

"Theodore!" Sam exclaimed. "What are you doing here?"

The attorney had a canteen slung over his arm and was carrying a valise.

"Didn't I mention I am the official judge? I must make sure everyone abides by the rules. I'll be roving about constantly the entire twenty-four hours."

"You'll be as worn out as the rest of us by the time this is done."

Pickleman set down the valise. "Not that I want to, mind you. It's yet another of your father's stipulations." He mopped his brow. "I suspect it's your father's way of needling me. He knew I am not much for physical exercise."

"It sounds like something Father would do, yes," Sam agreed.

"How big is the chest?" Fargo asked.

"I couldn't say," the attorney said. "I never saw it. He buried it before he came to me about revising the will."

"I wish he provided clues," Sam said wistfully.

"I would imagine," the lawyer said. "I tried to get more information out of him but all he did was smile and make that silly remark about whoever found it not having cause to weep."

"An understatement," Sam said.

"Yes, well." Pickleman picked up the valise. "I'm sorry but I must keep on the move. Good luck to you, Samantha. I have always liked you and I know you will treat your brothers and your sister more fairly than some of them would treat you."

"Thank you, Theodore."

Pickleman smiled and nodded and the vegetation swallowed him.

"A dedicated little man," Sam said. "He takes his responsibilities seriously and always performs them to the best of his ability."

Father was thinking about the chest. "Did your father get out in these woods much?"

"Hardly ever. He was too busy conducting business day in and day out. He brought a few clients out to the lodge from time to time and once and once only he went hunting with Roland, but that was about the extent of it." Sam paused. "Why did you ask?"

"If he didn't know these woods well," Fargo mused, "then odds are he didn't have a spot picked out ahead of time."

"So?"

"So he probably buried the chest at the first likely spot he came to."

"Likely how? Clear? Soft? Easy to remember?" Sam shook her head. "That's not much help."

Fargo was tired of being criticized. He felt he was onto something but exactly how it could help them eluded him. "Let's keep looking."

"Didn't I hear that you guide wagon trains from time to time? They must be in awe of your wood lore."

"Keep it up."

"I'm counting on you," Sam said with passion. "More than you can ever possibly realize."

"I'll do the best I can."

"Do better."

They resumed the hunt, Sam quiet and tense. As the minutes crawled into an hour and the hour into an hour and a half it became obvious, as Sam put it, that, "It's like looking for a needle in a haystack."

"We have twenty-four hours."

"For once my father was being generous. Or was he? He would like for us to experience twenty-four hours of sheer torture."

"Nice gent, your pa."

"No," Sam said sadly. "He was mean and cruel. To us, at any rate. I never did understand how he could blame us for Mother's death. It was an act of God."

"God does that a lot," Fargo said.

"Does what?"

"Kills people."

Sam chuckled. "What a strange thing to say. I doubt Father even believed. Mother died in a lot of pain, and I remember Father saying that any God who would let her suffer was either a lunatic or make-believe."

They poked into thickets. They checked behind boulders and around logs. They searched every shadowed nook. All with the same result.

They came to a rise and Samantha plopped down, her chin sinking to her chest. "I'm tired already. How about you?"

Fargo could go all day if he had to but he sat beside her and said, "Don't be so hard on yourself."

"So much is at stake." Sam plucked at the grass. "I'll never forgive Father for this. He couldn't divide up the inheritance and leave it at that. He had to turn it into a circus."

"Enough about the bastard."

Sam stopped plucking and leaned back. "I guess I do tend to go on about him. But you can't blame me under the circumstances."

Fargo scanned the forest: a mix of maple, oak and hickory. He was about to suggest they push on when he heard a faint cry to the south.

"Did you hear that?"

Nodding, Fargo stood. He listened but the seconds crawled by and the cry wasn't repeated.

"Did it sound like a call for help?"

Fargo couldn't say. It might have been. It might not. "Who else uses these woods besides your family?"

"Hardly a soul. Most people know this is private property." Sam moved to the end of the rise. "We should go have a look."

Fargo led. In over a hundred yards came out of the vegetation on the grassy bank of the creek. Here and there cottonwoods sprinkled the waterway, along with a few willows. "This have a name?"

"Clyborn Creek. My father named it after our family. It's a tributary of Bear Creek."

Fargo followed the bank west. The going was easier and they covered a lot of distance without seeing or hearing anyone.

"That water sure looks inviting."

Fargo agreed. He stepped to the edge of a knee-deep pool, cupped his hand, and dipped it in.

"I used to play in this creek when I was a girl." Samantha knelt beside him. "At least we don't have to worry about going thirsty."

Fargo sipped. Now all they had to do was find something so they wouldn't go hungry. He went to dip his hand in again when from out of the undergrowth came a low moan.

"Someone is hurt," Sam whispered.

Reaching up under his pant leg, Fargo palmed the Arkansas toothpick. On cat's feet he crept toward a patch of briars.

Samantha stayed at his side.

Fargo hoped the moan would be repeated but all he heard was the breeze rustling the trees. He circled along the thorns and went only a few steps when he saw part of a leg and a man's shoe poking out. From the way the grass was flattened and the briars broken and bent, it appeared the man had been heaved into them.

"Who is it?" Sam whispered, aghast.

Careful of the thorns, Fargo parted the branches. When he saw who it was, he quickly slid the toothpick under his belt, gripped the man's ankles, and pulled him out.

"Oh God!" Sam exclaimed, her hand flying to her throat. "Charles!"

Someone had got at her brother with a knife. His face had been slashed, his throat sliced, his sleeves cut to ribbons where he had used his arms to try to ward off the weapon. He had also been stabbed in the chest and the belly.

"Charles! Charles!" Sam threw herself down beside him. She touched his face and his chest and stared in horror at the blood on her hands. "Who would do such a thing?"

Fargo had a good idea. He felt for a pulse. There was one but it was weak and erratic. It didn't take a sawbones to know that Charles Clyborn wasn't long for this world.

"We must do something," Sam urged. "Run to the lodge and have them send for Dr. Williams in Hannibal. Hurry before it's too late."

"It already is."

"What? No, no, you're mistaken." Tears welled in Sam's eyes. She bent and gently touched his cheek. "Charles? Charles? Can you hear me? It's Samantha."

To Fargo's surprise, Charles's eyelids fluttered and opened. "Sam?" he croaked.

"Yes, Charles, yes." Sam hugged him and kissed his chin.

"Don't you worry. I'll have you carried to the lodge and we'll get Dr. Williams."

Charles tried to speak, couldn't, and tried again. "No," he rasped hoarsely. "It wouldn't do any good."

"Don't talk like that." Sam clasped his hand in hers. "I won't let anything happen to you."

"It already has." Charles coughed and a drop of blood trickled from a corner of his mouth. "Listen. I don't have much time."

"Oh, Charles," Sam said, and sobbed.

"A woman did this to me. I never saw her before. She came out of the trees and I said hello and she drew a knife and attacked me. I tried to defend myself but"—Charles stopped and coughed more violently. His gaze rose to Fargo— "I think she was the one you told us about. The woman who attacked you in Sam's bedroom."

"I figured it had to be her or her brother." Fargo scoured the surrounding greenery. "Where did she get to?"

"She tossed me into the pickers and walked off," Charles related. "The strangest thing is, she never said a word the whole time."

Fargo realized the female assassin could be watching them at that very moment. He kept his hand on the toothpick.

"I'll see that she pays," Sam said, tears trickling down her face. "I'll see that she's arrested and hung, so help me God."

Charles hadn't taken his eyes off Fargo. "Don't let them get Sam. Please. They'll do the same to her as they've done to me."

"Not if I can help it," Fargo vowed.

Charles smiled. "Thank you." He tried to raised his hand to Sam but was too weak. "One last thing."

"Don't talk. Save your strength."

"It's important." Charles took a long breath. "I found it."

In her sorrow and confusion, Sam said, "Found what?"

"Where Father buried the chest."

Sam gripped his shirt. "Did you dig it up? Did the woman who cut you take it with her?"

"No," Charles said. "I was on my way—" He stopped and his eyes widened and he said, "I'll be damned."

And he was gone.

15

Samantha slumped over her brother's body, buried her face in his shirt, and sobbed and sobbed.

Fargo didn't intrude on her grief. His every sense alert, he hunkered with his back to an oak. He couldn't shake the notion that the assassin was nearby, and half hoped she would attack them. Other than the cooing of a dove, the forest was uncommonly still, as if the wild things were holding their collective breaths waiting for the next explosion of violence.

Eventually Samantha stopped. Sniffing, she tenderly touched Charles's cheek. "We must tell Theodore. The body should be taken to the lodge and kept safe until we can hold a funeral."

"It might be best to leave him where he is until the hunt is over," Fargo suggested

"We leave him out here that long and the coyotes and buzzards will get hold of him."

"Not if we cover the body with tree limbs and brush."

"Not on your life," Samantha said.

Fargo understood her feelings but she wasn't thinking straight. "Pickleman can't call off the hunt. You heard him. Once it starts it can't be stopped."

Samantha spun. "Do you think I give a damn about my father and his insane will when my brother is lying here dead?"

"If you give up, whoever hired the woman who killed Charles will have gotten what they want."

"That's preposterous."

"Is it? Emmett dead. Charles dead. You out of the way. Who would want that? Who stands to gain the most?" Fargo didn't let her answer. "Tom, Roland, or Charlotte, that's who."

"I don't believe it for an instant."

"Think, damn it. One of your brothers or your sister had to hire Anders. One of them had to hire the other two assassins."

"No," Sam said, without much conviction. "There has to be another explanation."

"Like hell. Face the truth," Fargo bluntly declared. "Tom, Roland, or Charlotte. Two of those three are out to win the hunt no matter what it takes."

"They wouldn't do that."

"Tell Charles."

Samantha stared at her dead sibling and uttered a tiny whine of despair. Slumping, she covered her face with her hands. "Father, what in God's name have you done to us?"

Fargo rose to comfort her, and froze. Two figures had emerged from the trees. They glared at him and he glared back. "Sam," he said to warn her.

Sam lowered her arms. "Tom!" she exclaimed. "It's Charles! He's been murdered."

"So I see." Tom flicked a glance at the body. "It serves him right for being so pigheaded. I tried to talk him out of taking part but he wouldn't listen. He was as greedy as the rest of us."

"Oh, Tom," Sam said.

"Don't 'Oh Tom' me, damn you," Tom spat. "Charles and I never got along well. Would you have me pretend different now that he's dead?" He walked over and nudged the still form with his foot. "I can't say as I'll miss him much more than I miss Father, and I don't miss Father at all."

"How can you be so cold toward your own flesh and blood?"

"Oh, please," Tom said in disdain. "I'm as unlike the rest

of you as night from day. Father always suspected Mother was untrue to him, and to be frank, I tend to agree. For all we know, the stableman was my real father."

Sam was on her feet, her fists balled. "Don't you dare talk about Mother like that. Until the day she died she swore that you were hers and Father's and no one else's."

Tom shrugged. "Tramps always make excuses."

With a banshee cry, Samantha was on him. She punched at his face, at his eyes, and mouth. In her blind fury she missed more than she hit. Tom got his arms up to protect himself but was driven back. She clipped him on the temple and he staggered and might have fallen but Cletus Brun caught him and steadied him and then backhanded Sam.

It was hard to say who was more shocked, Sam, who reeled in pain, or Tom, who tore loose of Brun and shouted, "Don't hit her, you clod!"

"You're payin' me to protect you," Brun said.

"From paid killers. The ones who killed my brothers. Not from my own sister. I thought I made that clear."

By then Fargo reached them. He unleashed an uppercut that caught Brun full on the jaw and raised Brun onto the tips of his toes. Fargo landed a punch to the gut and another to the face. That would be enough to take most men down but it didn't take down Cletus Brun. The big Missourian snarled, raised fists the size of hams, and waded in.

"This time there's no holdin' back," he snarled.

That was fine by Fargo. He stood his ground and slugged it out. Knuckles grazed his cheek. A sledge slammed his shoulder. He flicked a jab, feinted, and drove his right fist into Brun's midsection. Brun grunted and took a step back. Fargo blocked a forearm, pivoted, and drove his fist into Brun's midsection a second time. Growling like an enraged bear, Cletus Brun flung his arms wide and sprang. Fargo was caught flatfooted. Before he could dodge he was enveloped in a bear hug and lifted off his feet.

"Now I have you, you son of a bitch."

Sam and Tom were yelling but Fargo couldn't hear what they were shouting for the roaring in his ears. He rammed his forehead at Brun's nose but the hulking brute had learned from their first fight and jerked his face around so his cheek took the brunt.

"Not this time."

Fargo's chest was a mass of pain. Brun had nearly cracked his ribs before; this time he might just succeed. Lowering his chin to his chest, Fargo whipped his head at Brun's chin. There was the *crunch* of teeth grinding together and wet drops spattered Fargo's face.

A hand appeared, tugging at Brun's arm. It was Samantha, shouting for Brun to let Fargo go. Tom ran up and pulled her away.

Fargo threw all his weight backward. He thought it would unbalance Brun and Brun would fall but the man's legs were as stout as redwoods. All Brun did was stagger a couple of steps and right himself.

"Nice try."

Brun grinned through the blood flecking his mouth, and tightened his hug. For Fargo, it was like having his chest caught in a massive vise. Bright dots pinwheeled before his eyes. His consciousness was fading. In desperation he did the only thing he could think of. He craned his neck and sank his teeth into Cletus Brun's ear.

Brun howled like a gut-shot wolf. He snapped his head back and in doing so lost his earlobe.

Fargo hadn't meant to bite it off. He tasted skin and blood and spit them out—into Brun's face. Brun was livid. Letting go, he seized Fargo by the throat and gouged his thick fingers deep.

"I'm going to kill you! Do you hear me? You're a dead man."

Fargo grabbed both wrists and tried to tear Brun's hands off but Brun was too strong. Once again bright lights sparkled like fireflies before Fargo's eyes. He punched at Brun's face, to no effect. He hit Brun in the stomach only to have Brun ignore the blows. Bit by bit the life was being strangled from him. It was do or die.

Fargo groped at his waist. His hand closed on the Arkansas toothpick.

Suddenly Samantha was there. She leaped on Brun's back and raked her fingernails across his face—across his eyes. Brun roared and flung her off. His grip slackened. Not much, but enough that Fargo was able to wrench his arm free and slash Brun across the cheek.

Brun slammed Fargo to the ground and retreated several steps. He touched his face and stared at the fresh blood glistening on his fingertips. Then he slipped his hand under his loose-fitting homespun shirt and when the hand reappeared it held an antler-handled knife with a blade inches longer than the toothpick. He took a step, then glanced at Sam and Tom Clyborn.

"Stay out of this or I'll kill you."

Fargo was breathing hard. He crouched, and when Brun came at him, slid out of the way. Brun wheeled and swung. Fargo threw himself back to keep from being decapitated.

The Missourian liked to talk when he fought. "It's you or me and it won't be me," he boasted.

Fargo sought to make him reckless by saying, "Come and try, you lump of lard."

It worked; Brun roared and attacked. His longer arms gave him an advantage. He could get in close but Fargo couldn't. Fargo tried several times and was forced back.

"Stop it!" Tom Clyborn yelled. "Stop it or you're fired!"

Apparently Brun didn't care. He lanced his knife at Fargo's face. Fargo ducked. He thrust his blade at Fargo's heart. Fargo skipped out of reach. Brun took a long stride and cleaved the air to split Fargo's skull and Fargo dodged and buried the toothpick to the hilt in Brun's side.

Brun grunted and jerked away. The scarlet that spurted

brought a cry of pain. He pressed his hand to the wound, the rage fading from his face.

"Damn you, little man."

Fargo stayed in a crouch, the toothpick low at his side, blood dripping from the blade to the grass.

Brun moved his hand and more scarlet flowed. Swaying slightly, he covered the hole and said, "I've had enough. I'm leavin'."

"Don't expect to be paid," Tom said.

Brun began to say something but stopped and looked at Fargo. "I'm goin' for the sawbones. It's over between you and me." He dropped his knife and started to turn.

"No," Fargo said.

Brun stopped. "You beat me. I'm bleedin' to death. If I don't hurry I might die."

"Who hired you?"

Brun licked his thick lips. "Tom, there."

"Who hired Anders and you," Fargo clarified.

"I don't know what you're talkin' about."

Fargo moved in front of him, blocking his way. "You want to go on lying, you can go on bleeding, too."

"Damn you."

"Skye," Sam said. "You don't have any proof. Let him go or his death will be on your conscience."

"I don't have a conscience," Fargo lied. But he wouldn't lose sleep over Cletus Brun. If Brun died it was on Brun's shoulders, not his.

"You heard her," the big Missourian said. "You ain't got any proof."

"You're not leaving until you tell me."

Tom intervened, saying, "This is absurd. I hired Brun. No one else."

"Stay out of this."

Brun tried to go around but Fargo again barred his path.

"Get out of my way."

"Who?"

"What makes you think you're right?"

"Anders said he had a partner. You're the only one who fits."

"You're guessin'."

"It's a good guess."

Brun glanced at the knife he had dropped but didn't try to pick it up. His side was stained and his fingers were covered with blood. "I don't have time for this."

"No, you don't," Fargo agreed. "Tell me and you can go for the doctor."

"You don't give an inch, do you?"

"Talk yourself to death if you want."

"All right." Brun swore some more, and looked at Tom and Sam. "It's true. Bucklin Anders and me were hired to see that none of you got that chest. I was to work on the inside and Anders was to shadow us and pick some of you off whenever he could."

"You miserable clod," Tom said.

"Who hired you?" Samantha echoed Fargo. "Was it Roland or Charlotte? They are the only two not here."

Brun grinned. "It will shock you, the one it is. You'd never have figured it in a million years."

"It was Roland then?"

"I'll tell you," Brun said. "I'll tell you and then I'm goin' for the doc." He paused, and opened his mouth.

At last, Fargo thought.

A shot boomed and a hole appeared in the center of Brun's forehead. His head snapped back and his huge frame shuddered. He collapsed without an outcry and lay twitching.

Fargo dropped down. He expected more shots but there were none. Pushing up, he ran toward the spot where he thought the shot came from. He saw no one. He heard no one. The undergrowth was so thick that the shooter could be hiding ten feet away and be invisible. Thwarted, Fargo went back.

"Anything?" Tom asked.

Fargo shook his head.

"Wonderful. Whoever it was might kill one of us next."

Samantha was by Charles, her head bowed in sorrow. "Whoever it is, they won't stop until they have what they're after. I'm afraid the worst is yet to come."

So did Fargo.

16

Fargo was wiping the toothpick clean on Brun's shirt when the underbrush rustled. He spun, thinking the killer was going to try and finish the job but it was Theodore Pickleman, sweaty from running and clutching his valise as if afraid he would drop it.

"I thought I heard a shot," the lawyer began, and saw the two bodies. "Oh, my word. What on Earth has happened?"

Samantha told him, and gestured at her fallen brother. "We have to call off the hunt. We can conduct it again after Charles's funeral."

"No, my dear, we can't," Pickleman said, shaking his head. "Your father was explicit. Once begun, the hunt can't be stopped, not for any reason. I'm afraid that you must see it through to the end or forfeit your chance at the inheritance."

"But Charles is *dead*," Sam practically shouted. "Call everyone in and we'll tend to the body and then start over again."

"Haven't you listened to a word I've said? I can't do that. It's not permitted."

"To hell with the inheritance."

"Speak for yourself, sister," Tom told her. "I, for one, am not giving up until the chest is mine. I refuse to forfeit."

"I'm afraid you already have," Pickleman said.

Tom whirled on him. "What the hell are you talking about? I've done no such thing."

Pickleman sighed and put his hands to his temples and

rubbed them. "I swear. This ordeal is giving me a headache. How many times must I repeat myself? Or didn't you hear me when I read the clause about no weapons?"

"I don't have any," Tom said.

The lawyer pointed at the knife that lay near Cletus Brun. "He had one. He broke the rules, and if he were alive I would disqualify him from taking part."

"I didn't know he had it."

"Maybe you didn't, maybe you did. The point is that Mr. Brun was your partner, and if one is disqualified, so is the other."

"The hell you say."

"I'm afraid you are out of the running for the inheritance," Pickleman informed him. "You and Samantha might as well wait at the hunting lodge until this is over."

"Me?" Sam said.

Pickleman pointed at Fargo. "Is that or is that not a knife I see in your partner's hand? What applies to your brother equally applies to you. Both of you are out of the hunt."

Tom walked up to the attorney. "Think again."

"Be reasonable. I'm only doing what your father required of me." Pickleman smiled and placed his hand on Tom's shoulder. "Put yourself in my shoes and I'm sure you'll understand."

Tom swatted the hand off. "No, you put yourself in ours. You never said anything about both partners being removed if one broke the rules. I won't stand for it. Either Sam and I continue or we'll hire another attorney and sue you, you bastard."

"Now, now. No name calling." Pickleman appealed to Samantha. "Talk to him. Make him understand."

"I agree with Tom on this," Sam said. "You never explained any of this at supper last night. I refuse to be blamed for Fargo having a knife. I didn't even know he had one on him."

"That's true," Fargo spoke up.

"Be that as it may . . ." Pickleman began, and got no further.

Lunging, Tom grabbed him by the shirt and shook him, hard. "You listen, and you listen good, you little weasel. Murders have been committed. If I have to, I'll send for the sheriff and I can damn well guarantee that *he* will stop the hunt whether you want him to or not."

"That would complicate things."

"You don't know the half of it. It wouldn't surprise me if he raised a posse and scoured these woods for the killers and then made each of us go to his office for questioning. It could be a week or more before you can hold another hunt, if he even lets you."

"It's in the will. The sheriff can't stop it."

"He can go to a judge and have the judge stop it," Tom predicted. "Then where will you be? No hunt, no way to settle the inheritance except in court. The case could be tied up for years."

Pickleman looked worried. "I wouldn't want that. The cost to the estate would be enormous."

"There's even a chance the judge might declare the will invalid. And you couldn't do a thing about it."

Prying at Tom's hand, Pickleman said, "Please. Let go of me. You've made your point."

"I'm not disqualified?"

"No. Neither is Sam. I'll permit both of you to continue under two conditions."

Sam asked suspiciously, "What are they?"

"First, that neither of you tell anyone I broke the rules for your benefit. It could cause all sorts of trouble for me, legally."

Tom shrugged. "All I care about is staying in the hunt. What's the second condition?"

"While I am willing to reinstate the two of you, I can't reinstate Mr. Fargo. He's out, and that's final."

"No," Sam said.

"Come on, Samantha." Pickleman was growing flustered. "I'm trying to meet you halfway. You could at least do the same."

"I need him."

"He has a *knife*."

"That's easily remedied." Sam walked over to Fargo and held out her hand. "You'll get it back, after."

Fargo was loath to part with the toothpick. It left him unarmed, with two killers out there somewhere.

"Please, Skye. It's the only way."

With great reluctance Fargo placed it in her hand. "Hell."

Sam turned and held the toothpick out to Pickleman. "Take this. Problem solved. He doesn't have a weapon and can continue as my partner."

"You're making a mockery of the will," Pickleman complained, but he put the toothpick in his valise. "Carry on as you were. I'll arrange for these bodies to be taken to the lodge and will hold them there until the hunt is over."

Sam smiled and patted his cheek. "I knew I could count on you, Theodore. You've always been a friend as well as our counselor."

"To you, perhaps, but to your father I was never anything but his lawyer. Another menial to be bossed around as he saw fit."

"He confided things in you he never confided in the rest of us."

"Only because he knew my lips were sealed against ever revealing his secrets. There's such a thing as attorney-client privilege." Pickleman regarded the bodies. "Off you go. There's a lot I must get done and still do my duty as monitor of this horrible hunt."

"Even you agree it's wrong," Sam said.

"But not for the same reasons." Pickleman gazed at the wall of green. "Let me see. Which direction would the lodge be?" He started walking to the east.

"Not that way," Fargo said, and extended his arm in the

direction the lawyer should go. "The lodge is that way. To the northwest."

"Thank you. But if you don't mind my asking, how can you tell which is which?"

Fargo squinted up at the sun. "There's all the help you need. It rises in the east and sets in the west. Remember that and you can never get lost."

"Maybe you can't but I can." Pickleman gazed uncertainly skyward. "What about north and south?"

"It's early yet so the sun is still in the eastern half of the sky," Fargo explained. "Raise your left arm and point at it. Like that. Now raise your right arm. Your left is pointing east, your right is pointing west, your face is to the north and your backside to the south."

"How do you remember all that? And what if it happens to be the afternoon and the sun is to the west?" Pickleman shook his head. "I would make a sorry plainsman. Give me my law books any day." He hurried off in the right direction.

Sam said to Tom, "Thank you for standing up for us and getting him to change his mind."

Tom laughed. "I didn't do it for you, stupid. I did it for me. I couldn't very well demand he permit me to continue the hunt and not you when both our partners broke the rules." He headed off. "Now if you'll excuse me, there's a chest I need to find."

"He'll never change," Sam said.

Fargo was thinking of the toothpick and his Colt. Thank God it wasn't the Rockies where he'd have to be on the lookout for roving grizzlies and painted hostiles.

Sam looked down at her hands. She gave a slight shudder and said in horror, "I just noticed. I have Charles's blood on me."

"Wash it off. I'll keep watch." Fargo turned his back to the creek and assumed she would do as he suggested. Instead, she came over and stood so close to him, her breasts brushed his arm.

"Do you know what would be wonderful right about now?"

"For you to have a six-gun hid under your dress."

"No, silly. A bath."

All Fargo could do was stare.

"Why are you looking at me like that? I'm sweaty and smelly and I have blood on me. What's more natural than to take a bath? That pool is deep enough. We could sit and let the water wash over us. It will be grand."

"We?"

"You can't expect me to do it alone. Shed your buckskins and join me. It won't take long."

Fargo glanced at Charles and then at Brun and then at the shadowed woods and finally at her. "Was everyone in your family born with empty space between their ears?"

"Whoever stabbed my brother and shot that oaf are long gone. Please. I really want to wash this blood off."

"You can jump in the creek if you want but not me." Fargo had credited her with more common sense. "I like breathing too much."

"All right, then. Be that way." Sam flounced to the bank and slid down to the water's edge where she began stripping with her back to him.

Fargo moved to a log and sat facing the woods. He heard her mutter, and grinned. His grin died when he thought he spied movement off in the undergrowth. He tensed and braced for the crack of another shot.

The vegetation parted and a brown shape stepped timidly into view. It was a doe, her ears up, looking right and left. She had caught his scent but didn't know where he was.

"Howdy, girl."

That was all it took. Wheeling, she showed her tail and bolted in long leaps that swiftly carried her out of sight.

"What did you say?" Samantha asked.

"I wasn't talking to you."

"You were talking to yourself? And you accused me of having space between my ears."

Fargo chuckled. Her dander was up. Most females took criticism about as well as most males took being called yellow. He glanced back and saw her bare back and her luxurious hair falling past her shoulders and entertained a notion he shouldn't. "No," he said out loud.

"What was that? Or are you talking to yourself again?"

"Hurry up and wash and get dressed," Fargo said more gruffly than he intended.

"I'll thank you not to be so bossy. I hired you, remember? Not the other way around."

Fargo heard her wade out.

"Goodness, this water is cold. I have gooseflesh all over me."

"No," Fargo said again.

"I beg your pardon? You'll have to speak up."

Fargo fought with himself, and lost. He shifted on the log so he could see her and the forest, both. "Oh God," he breathed.

Samantha had reached the middle of the pool. Sunlight played over her superb body, showing every detail: the velvet sheen of her neck, the upturned peaks on her twin mounds, her flat tummy, and bushy thatch and smooth thighs. She bent and dipped her hands in the water and her breasts jiggled. Her bottom was two smooth moons.

"No," Fargo said, more quietly than before.

"The water is so clear I can see the bottom. There are small fish in here. And I saw a frog on the other side." Sam went on splashing.

Fargo couldn't take his eyes off her. He felt himself stir, and whispered to himself, "No, damn me."

"Now that I'm getting used to the water it's not bad," Sam informed him while slowly sinking in to her waist. She splashed water on her neck and her breasts and giggled girlishly. "I needed this."

Fargo imagined one of her nipples in his mouth, and stood.

Self-preservation battled lust and lust won. With a last glance at the vegetation, he moved to the top of the bank.

"Don't tell me you've changed your mind?"

Fargo sat and tugged on a boot. "If we get killed it will be your fault."

Samantha cupped water in both hands, placed her hands on her breasts, and slowly rubbed. "If you come in, you must promise to behave yourself."

"Like hell," Skye Fargo said.

17

There were times when a man knew he was making a mistake but he made it anyway. Times when a man knew he was being as dumb as a tree stump but he couldn't help himself. Times when a tiny voice in the back of his mind warned, "Don't do this!" and he did it. Times when, like now, Fargo wanted to kick himself. He stripped off his boots and clothes and hat and waded into the pool. It came only as high as his knees. The bottom was slippery, mud and a few loose rocks, and he stepped with care. His skin rippled with goose bumps. He shivered slightly.

"Told you it was cold."

Fargo's eyes were glued to her breasts. She was still rubbing them, a silent invite in her eyes. A mocking invite, if her grin meant anything. "I was wrong about you," he said."

"In what way?"

"You're just like every other woman I've ever met."

"You thought I wasn't?"

"For a while there I thought you never let your feelings get the better of you."

Samantha laughed. "Silly man. Women always think with their hearts and not with their heads."

"I'll try to remember that." By then Fargo reached her. A gnawing ache in his loins bore testimony to his need. He reached out and cupped her right breast. It was wet and smooth and the nipple hardened when he pinched it.

"Oh," Sam said softly.

Fargo glanced over his shoulder at the woods. Either of the assassins, or both, could be near. To hell with it, he thought, and gave Sam his undivided attention.

Her eyelids were hooded. The pink tip of her tongue rimmed her red lips. "Don't stop."

Fargo cupped her other breast and kneaded both. Under the water his manhood twitched and stirred and firmed. His need became an irresistible urge. He pulled her to him and kissed her. Their tongues met. Their bodies touched. The wet of the water added an extra sensation. He felt his pole rub her thigh and his lust became complete. "Damn, I want you," he said when they broke for breath.

"You make it sound like a bad thing," Sam teased.

"This is the same as poking my head into a grizzly's den."

"I'm a smelly old bear?" Samantha giggled.

"You're bare, all right," Fargo said, and applied his mouth to her neck, to her throat, to her ear.

Sam mewed and ground herself against him, the while her hands explored his back and his buttocks and one of them slid around and down to grip his member. "Oh, I do so love this."

It was what Fargo lived for. For some men it was money. For other men it was power. Some men it was other pursuits, like horse breeding or hunting or fishing or any of a thousand things. Not him. He lived for females. In his eyes nothing could hold a candle to the feel of ramming his pole into a willing woman.

Fargo took her standing up. He caressed and molded and kissed until she was hot with desire and her need as keen as his own. Then he parted her legs and had her grip him by the shoulders and raise up, and in one swift movement, he impaled her.

Samantha gasped and threw her head back. The windows to her soul shone with pure pleasure. "Yesssssss. Like that."

Fargo rocked on his heels. He had to be careful, as slippery as it was. The feel of her hot sheath and the cool water and the air on his skin were like a potent drug. The tiny voice yelled at him to stop and he smothered it. "Some things a man just has to do," he said to himself.

"Ummmmm?" Sam's eyes were closed and she matched his thrusts with swirls of her pelvis.

Fargo devoted himself to pounding her. His mouth, his hands, were everywhere. It wasn't long before she moved faster and harder and he could tell she was near the brink. To send her over he slid a hand down between them and rubbed her swollen knob. It was all it took.

Sam exploded, churning the pool with the violence of her release. "Huh! Huh! Huh!" she gasped.

Fargo let himself go. He rammed up and in and it felt as if his insides were being ripped from his body. The pool roiled, the water lapped at them in small wavelets. It went on and on until finally she was spent and sagged against him and he was spent and suddenly tired.

"God, you're good," Sam whispered. She slowly lowered her legs and leaned against him. "I'm as weak as a kitten."

Fargo scooped her into his arms and carried her to the bank. He set her down on the grass and lay next to her, his arm for her pillow. He closed his eyes. The tiny voice was at it again but the bank partially hid them so he was content to lie there a while.

"Skye?"

"Mmmm?" Fargo wanted her to be quiet but it wasn't to be.

"May I ask you a question?"

"I can't stop the moon and the sun from rising, either."

"What? Oh." Sam gave a throaty laugh. "Very well. Who do you think it is?"

Fargo sighed and opened his eyes. "Who what?"

"Who hired Brun and that Anders fellow? Who hired the brother and sister? I know it's not me so it has to be Tom, Roland or Charlotte. I would guess Tom hired Brun and Anders even though he denies it. That leaves Roland or Charlotte to have hired the other two."

"Could be."

"I can't see Roland doing it, though. He's too nice."

"Tom is right about one thing. When there's a lot of money at stake, nice doesn't always count for much."

"I still think it has to be Charlotte. My sweet little sister has always had a hard edge. She hides it well but it's there, just under the surface. I've often thought she would make a good wildcat."

Fargo grinned and nipped her ear. "You make a fine wildcat yourself."

"Oh, you." Sam kissed his cheek. "I can't help myself. You bring it out of me, somehow."

After that she lay still. Fargo closed his eyes again and was about to doze off when a twig snapped. He heard it as clear as anything. He raised his head and saw that Sam had heard it, too, and was tense with apprehension. Putting a finger to his lips, he slid his arm out from under her and edged to the top.

The woods seemed undisturbed but something, or someone, had stepped on that twig. Fargo watched and waited but nothing showed and after a few minutes he slid back down. "Get dressed."

"Who was it?"

"I don't even know if it was a who."

"I'm glad you're with me. I don't know as I could take this if I were by myself. I've always thought of myself as brave, but this—"

Fargo put his finger to her lips. "Get dressed," he repeated, and hurriedly donned his buckskins, boots and hat.

Sam was slower but only because she had so many buttons and more garments. "I'm ready," she finally whispered.

The woods appeared peaceful. Fargo reached down and said, "Grab my wrist." When she did, he hauled her up beside him and then over the top of the bank. Still holding on to her, he crouched and moved along the bank and into a stand of cottonwoods. Hunkering next to a trunk, he said quietly, "From here on out we don't take chances. You stay close.

We don't make noise if we can help it. When I stop, you stop. If I drop flat, you drop flat. Savvy?"

"I love it when you're forceful."

Fargo could have slapped her. He took hold of her shoulders and they locked eyes. "No more games. Emmett and Charles are dead and I don't care to join them."

"I was only joking."

"No more. We're being hunted. We stay sharp or we're dead."

"You really believe that? About being hunted, I mean?"

"The only way whoever hired those killers can be sure of claiming the inheritance is if the rest of you are dead."

"But no one can be sure unless they find the chest."

"It ups their odds."

"I suppose. And later, if they don't find the chest, they can contest the will in court as the sole surviving heir."

"I don't give a damn about why they want us dead," Fargo said. "It's enough that they do. And I don't die easy."

Sam started to reply but Fargo hushed her with a gesture. He thought he'd heard something. He probed the shadows dappling the green but saw nothing out of the ordinary. "You'll do as I say?"

"We have an accord," Sam said, and grinned.

Over the next several hours they spent every minute searching. They paralleled the creek until they came to a tree with a red patch of paint, marking the boundary of the search area. They crisscrossed the woods. They poked into thickets and under leaves and moved logs.

By the position of the sun it was about two in the afternoon when Fargo came to the base of a low bluff. It offered shade and concealment, and he sat and put his elbows on his knees and his chin in his hands. "We're not getting anywhere."

"Don't give up. We have until six tomorrow morning." Sam placed a hand at the small of her back and wearily sank beside him. "By then I'll be so sore and tired, I'll hardly be able to move."

"You'll need to sleep eventually."

"Not if I can help it. I intend to stay up all night searching, if it comes to that."

"In the dark we'd need torches." Fargo didn't add that it would make them easy targets.

"I wish Father had given us clues. He's asking the impossible. There's too much ground to cover and most of it wooded."

Fargo had a thought. "Maybe he made it so hard because he didn't want any of you to find the damn chest."

Sam pursed her lips. "You know, that would be just like him. He hated us enough. A cruel jest on his part. Yes, he would like that very much." She sighed. "What really rankles is that if none of us find the thing, the entire estate goes to charity." Sam caught herself. "Not that I have anything against giving money to the poor. To the contrary. I've done it myself. But Father never did. He used to say that the poor deserved their fate, that if they had any drive and any grit, they wouldn't be poor to begin with."

"Like I said before, nice gent, your father."

"No, Skye. He was anything but. He was mean and hurtful and despicable at times. A fluke of fate turned him from a loving father into a monster."

They both stiffened at the sudden snap and crackle of brush. Out of it came two figures, their dresses showing wear and tear, their shoes sprinkled with dust and dirt.

"Sam!" Charlotte exclaimed, and smiled. She nudged Amanda and the pair came over. "I take it you're not having any better luck than we are?"

Samantha shook her head.

"I swear, we've covered every square foot," Charlotte said, and her cousin nodded. "I thought that all we had to do was find a spot where someone had dug but it's not that simple."

"Charlotte, brace yourself," Sam said softly.

"Why?"

"Charles is dead."

Charlotte took a step back and paled. "No. Not him." Tears welled at the corners of her eyes. "How did it happen?"

"He was stabbed to death."

"God no."

To Fargo her shock seemed genuine. But some people were good actors and she might be one.

"That's not all." Sam told her about Cletus Brun. Both Charlotte and Amanda glanced at Fargo but neither said anything until Sam was done.

"Then Tom is on his own?" Charlotte smiled. "Good. It serves him right. Of all of us, I want Tom to win the least."

Amanda asked, "What about Roland? Have you seen any sign of him?"

"No."

"Neither have we," Charlotte said. "I hope he's all right." She looked at her sister and at Fargo and bit her lower lip.

"What?" Sam prompted.

"I've had a lot of time to think and I was wondering—" Charlotte stopped. "No, you probably wouldn't agree."

"Agree to what? Speak up."

Charlotte swept an arm at the ring of forest. "I don't like these woods. They're spooky. I'll like them even less once the sun goes down. If we haven't found the chest by then, I was wondering if you would want to join forces?"

"You always were afraid of the dark."

"Fine. Poke fun at me. I just thought it would be safer for all of us if we were together." Charlotte started to turn.

"Hold on. I wasn't poking fun. It makes sense. But why wait until nightfall? Why not stick together from here on out and if we find the chest we agree to split the inheritance between us?"

"You mean that?" Charlotte asked hopefully.

"As you say, there's safety in numbers. I'm sure Fargo agrees. Don't you, Skye?"

Fargo was about to answer when a rifle barrel poked out of the trees.

18

Fargo had been watching the woods the whole time. He saw the barrel the instant it appeared and he acted in the same heartbeat. "Get down!" he bellowed, and flung himself flat even as he pulled Samantha with him. The rifle thundered. He heard a thwack and twisted toward Sam, thinking she had been shot. But she hadn't.

Amanda had been hit in the back of the head. The slug ruptured her face, taking part of her nose and cheek with it. She was still on her feet but her eyes were empty of life and her legs starting to give way.

"Amanda!" Charlotte cried. She was riveted in horror and dismay.

"Down, damn it!" Fargo lunged, wrapped an arm around her ankles, and yanked at the very moment that the rifle belched lead and smoke a second time.

The killer missed.

Fargo had Sam on one side and Charlotte on the other. They couldn't stay there; they were too exposed. "Run!" he commanded, and since he couldn't count on them to obey, he grabbed both and raced around the bluff, pulling them. Sam matched him but Charlotte dug in her heels.

"Amanda! I can't leave her!"

"She's dead!" Fargo pulled harder. They would be dead, too, if they didn't find cover, and quickly. He rounded the bluff as another shot struck a tree and flew another twenty feet, veering back and forth to make it harder for the shooter to hit them. The next instant they plunged into heavy cover.

The vegetation was so dense that Fargo doubted the killer could see them but he wasn't taking chances. A spruce flanked by high weeds offered haven. He flattened and tugged the women down beside him.

"Amanda," Charlotte said, and sobbed.

"Quiet." Fargo let go and raised his head high enough to see over the weeds. There was no sign of pursuit but it could be the shooter was too smart to show him or her self.

"What do we do?" Sam whispered. "We can't fight a rifle with our bare hands."

Fargo was all too aware of that. He looked around for a downed tree limb or a fist-sized rock.

"Why did they shoot Amanda?" Sam wondered. "Why not Charlotte or me? Amanda can't inherent anything."

"Maybe they're toying with us," Fargo speculated. "Or maybe they were aiming at Charlotte or you and Amanda stepped into their sights." He hadn't been paying attention to what Amanda was doing.

"We must report this," Charlotte said, tears moistening her cheeks. "We must get to the hunting lodge and send word to the sheriff."

"I agree," Sam said.

Fargo rose up for another look around. He couldn't see much for all the trees. The lodge had to be a quarter of a mile away, maybe more. Reaching it would take some doing.

"Well?" Charlotte prompted.

Fargo squatted. "It could be that's what they want us to do. Panic and run for the lodge and right into their guns."

"You don't know that."

"I'm a good guesser."

Sam said, "Our other option is to stay put. The shots were bound to be heard. Pickleman will come. Or maybe Roland or Tom."

"If they're still alive," Fargo said.

Charlotte hissed in anger. "First Emmett and then Charles and now Amanda. I want to find the vermin who killed them. I want to see them suffer for what they've done."

"It's a pity we weren't allowed weapons," Sam said.

Fargo had never missed his Colt and Henry more. This was why he never went anywhere without them. In times of danger a gun was a man's best friend.

"Do we try for the lodge or not?" Charlotte asked.

"We try," Fargo replied. "But we do it my way." He lowered onto his belly and crabbed backward. "Do as I do. And from here on out no talking unless I say it's safe."

The sisters mimicked him. Charlotte's dress snagged on a rock and she started to swear but stopped at a sharp gesture from Fargo. He was a ghost compared to them. He glided along making very little sound; they made a lot. It didn't help that their dresses kept catching on the brush, or that Charlotte kept swatting at a fly.

Fargo halted after only a hundred feet. "We're making it too easy for them," he whispered.

"What are you talking about?" Charlotte asked.

Samantha understood. "I can't help it. I try to be quiet but I don't have much practice at it."

"We should wait for dark," Fargo proposed.

"And leave poor Amanda lying back there for the coyotes to eat?" Charlotte shook her head. "I should say not."

"They'll feed on you, too, if we're not more careful."

"Look. It's not that far to the lodge. All we have to do is reach it and we're safe." Charlotte began to rise and jerked her arm away when Fargo went to stop her. "I'm tired of skulking about. Let's run for it and to hell with the assassins."

From out of nowhere streaked a knife. Spinning end over end, it struck Charlotte in the chest with a sickening *thuck*. The blade buried itself to the hilt. She cried out and clutched it.

"No!" Fargo said.

Charlotte wrenched on the knife. It came out—and so did a fountain of scarlet, spurting like water from a hose. She gasped and tottered and bleated, "God, not me, too." With that she toppled.

"Charlotte!" Samantha scrambled to scoop her sister into her arms but Fargo was quicker. He scooped Sam into his and darted in among a cluster of pines. She fought him but he held fast, saying into her ear, "Do you want to wind up like her?"

Sam went limp. She sobbed and covered her mouth and then pressed her face to him and cried.

Fargo let her. The pines protected them for the moment. He was sorry about Charlotte but she had been too stubborn for her own good. Her death meant Tom or Roland had hired the brother and sister killers. Or did it? The pair had killed Anders. The pair had killed Cletus Brun, Tom's partner in the hunt. That made it unlikely Tom had hired them. Which left one person, the one he never would have suspected, the one he had liked from the start since they had so much in common. "I'll be damned."

"What?" Sam asked through her tears.

"Nothing." Fargo figured she had endured enough in the past few minutes. The revelation could wait.

Sam sat up. She sniffled and wiped her sleeve across her face. "Do you think they're still out there?"

"At least one of them is."

"I bet you could make it to the lodge without me to slow you down."

"No."

"I don't want you to die on my account."

"This isn't about you," Fargo told her. "It's not about your brothers or your sister or the chest your father buried. It hasn't been since the steamboat."

"Then what?" Sam asked in puzzlement.

"It's about *me*. Those bastards tried to kill me on the *Yancy*. That made it personal. You could say you want to be shed of me as your partner right this second and I wouldn't leave. I'm not going anywhere until I've paid them back."

"An eye for an eye—is that your creed?"

"You're goddamn right it is." Fargo was growing angrier the more he talked. Reining in his temper, he finished with, "I'm in this to the end whether you want me to be or not."

Her hand found his. "I couldn't make it without you."

Off in the woods something moved. Fargo caught a glimpse. He doubted it was a deer. Putting a finger to his lips, he backed away and motioned for her to follow.

For one of the few times since Fargo met her, fright showed in Samantha's eyes. She had lost two brothers and seen her sister killed and she knew she might be next. He didn't blame her for being scared.

It was cat and mouse and they were the mice. Fargo could never be sure they had given their stalker the slip. He stayed low, always hugging the shadows, always staying close to trees and thickets so the assassin wouldn't have a clear shot or be able to throw another knife.

They had been at it for nearly ten minutes when Fargo drew up short. Up ahead the undergrowth moved. Either the killer had circled around in front of them or it was an animal. But he was wrong.

Out of the vegetation came Tom Clyborn. He was searching the ground and hadn't seen them. He was so close that when he did, he gave a start and blurted, "Sam! Fargo! Why didn't you say something?"

Fargo seized Tom's forearm and forcibly pulled him down. Tom resisted and opened his mouth to object but Fargo clamped his other hand over it. "One of the killers is after us. Keep still and keep your voice down."

Tom desisted. When Fargo removed his hand he whispered, "You're being stalked?"

Sam nodded.

"I haven't seen hide nor hair of anyone since I left you earlier. Have you seen any of the others?"

"Charlotte and Amanda," Sam said, and sorrowfully informed him, "They're both dead."

"Charlotte too?" Tom bowed his head. "Damn it. Now there are only three of us left."

"So far as we know."

"Eh? Oh. You mean Roland might be dead, too?" Tom gazed about. "Where's the killer? Which one is it, Fargo? The man or the woman you told us about?"

"It could be either. Or both."

"I hope it's the woman. She'll be easier to fight."

Fargo remembered how skilled the mystery woman was with a knife and how she hopped around like a jackrabbit. "I wouldn't count on that if I were you. They're both good at what they do."

"What's your plan?"

Sam said, "We're trying to reach the hunting lodge. Pickleman needs to be told, and whether he wants to or not, I'm getting word to the sheriff and we're ending this stupid hunt once and for all. The will be damned."

"Damn Father, you mean," Tom said. "This is all his fault. Him and his hate for us."

Fargo broke in with, "We must keep on the move."

"Lead the way," Tom said. "I don't have any idea where the lodge is."

Fargo nodded and went to start off when an idea struck him. He scanned the forest and said half to himself, "It might work."

"What might?" Sam asked.

"I thought we are heading for the lodge?" Tom said.

"The killer might not know you're with us," Fargo explained. "If the two of you go on alone, he might think it's your sister and me."

"What about you?" Tom wanted to know.

"I'll climb a tree. When I see who it is, I'll stalk them like they've been stalking us. When I'm close I'll jump them and kill them and the two of you will be safe."

"I like it," Sam said.

"I don't," Tom declared. "What if you don't spot them? What if they catch on that you're stalking them and jump you instead? Or what if they decide to kill us before you jump them?" He shook his head. "There's too much that can go wrong."

"None of us might not reach the hunting lodge if we don't do something."

"I'll take my chances. I say we stick together."

"Please, Tom," Sam said. "You're being stubborn."

"You're damn right I am. My life is at stake."

"I trust Skye, Tom. He's doing all he can to keep us alive."

"So it's *Skye*, is it?" Tom smirked. "If you want to trust him, go right ahead. But don't expect me to."

"Be reasonable, will you?"

"The three of us should stick together," Tom insisted. "I'll watch your backs and you watch mine."

Fargo bit off an impulse to swear a blue streak. They couldn't afford to stay there squabbling. "I know you hired Brun and Anders."

"What?"

"I know you hired them and the sheriff will want to know, too. But I'll keep my mouth shut if you'll do as your sister wants."

"You son of a bitch."

"Well?"

"Well nothing," Tom spat. "For your information I *didn't* have anything to do with Anders and I hired Brun to help me in the hunt and nothing more."

Fargo almost believed him. But if Tom didn't hire them, who did? Roland? And if Roland hired them, who hired the brother and sister?

"Will you do it if I beg you?" Sam asked her brother.

"I might have. But not now. Not after your scout has insulted me. We're sticking together and that's final."

"You heard Skye. The killer will catch us."

"You're already caught," said a voice.

Fargo spun.

It was the brother. He stood six feet away, a Remington revolver in his hand. "I should thank you for making it so easy."

19

Tom Clyborn started to stand but the click of the revolver's hammer turned him to stone. "Don't!" he bleated, throwing his hands in front of him as if to ward off searing lead.

Fargo didn't twitch a muscle. He knew how deadly this killer and his sister were.

The young man showed no more emotion than a rock. He said in a cold tone with the same hint of an accent Fargo had noticed before, "I do so hate cowards. Sit down, fool, and keep your hands where I can see them. The same applies to both of you," he addressed Fargo and Samantha.

Fargo sank but he contrived to coil his legs under him. He placed his hands in plain sight.

"Who are you?" Samantha asked. "What do you want?"

"Don't be stupid," the young man said. "Someone in my line of work doesn't ever say who they are. As to what I want, my work speaks for itself."

"You're an assassin," Sam said.

"For want of a better word, yes." The man took a step to the left, the Remington unwavering. "I don't flatter myself when I say we are two of the best there are at what we do."

"We?"

Fargo said, "Him and his sister."

The assassin's dark eyes flitted to Fargo. "You remember us, do you?" he sarcastically asked.

"Folks who try to kill me tend to stick in my mind."

A hint of a smile touched the young man's mouth. "Forty-three times we've been hired, and you are the only person we've ever failed to kill. Your reflexes are the fastest we've ever seen."

Fargo said nothing.

"Who hired you?" Sam asked. "Will you tell us that much at least?"

"My employer will make himself known soon enough. He desires to talk to you before we finish it."

"What about?"

"He didn't say but I suspect it is the chest that your père"—the young man caught himself—"sorry, the chest that your father buried." He paused. "You haven't found it yet, have you?"

"If I had I wouldn't be sitting here," Tom said. "I'd be claiming what is rightfully mine."

"To you it is everything, yes?"

"Of course. We're talking millions of dollars." Tom swore. "And you called *me* a fool."

"You are a family of fools," the assassin said. "There is enough money for all of you. You could have agreed to work together to find the chest and divide the money between you. But no. In your greed each of you thought to be the only one to inherit." The young man shook his head. "Such a waste."

"Who the hell are *you* to judge us? You kill for a living, for God's sake."

"*Oui*. An honorable profession, despite what you might think."

Sam said, "Where is the honor in killing?"

"The honor is in how it is done. My sister and I are well respected in our small fraternity for always fulfilling the terms of a contract."

"When I get my hands on Roland," Tom said.

The assassin glanced into the trees. He took a gold pocket watch from a pocket and opened it and checked the time. Closing the watch, he put it back. Then he pointed the Remington at the ground and fired twice.

"What on Earth?" Samantha blurted.

"It's a signal," Fargo said.

The assassin nodded. "*Oui*. You are as smart as you are fast. I wonder. You have it figured out by now, do you not?"

"I reckon I'm not as smart as you think," Fargo said dryly.

The young man smiled. "It is diabolical. I would not have thought of such a thing but then I have too much honor."

"There you go again," Tom scoffed. "You and your honor. You don't know the meaning of the word."

"Were that true, you despicable wretch, you would already be dead."

Tom started to respond but the young killer motioned with the Remington and said, "I have listened to enough. You will keep your mouth shut until they get here."

"May I ask you a question?" Sam politely inquired.

"*Oui*."

"Was it you or your sister who shot my brother Emmett?"

"The youngest one? Neither of us. It was the man called Anders."

"And my other brother, Charles? Was it your sister who cut him to ribbons?"

"My sister. She likes to work with knives. She likes to cut and see the blood."

"My cousin Amanda? And my sister Charlotte? Who murdered them?"

"They were my kills."

"You feel no remorse?"

"For me it is a job. I have no feelings one way or the other. I kill and I am paid and that is all there is."

"God," Samantha said.

"How can you believe after all that has happened?" the young man asked her. "Be mature. There is no *Dieu*, no God. It is a fiction told children so they will not be scared of the dark."

"You're a monster."

"I have been called that before. I take it as a compliment.

I would rather see life for what it is than live as another of the sheep."

"You have a low opinion of your fellow man."

"It could not be lower," the young assassin said.

"What happened to make you this way? Surely there must be a shred of decency somewhere deep inside of you?"

"You are a silly woman."

Tom said, "How much are you and your sister being paid?"

"I told you not to talk."

"Hear me out on this. It will be worth your while." Tom leaned toward him. "Whatever you're being paid to kill us, I'll pay you double not to. Hell, I'll pay you triple."

"Where would you get the money? It is my understanding you have very little of your own."

"When I win the inheritance—"

The young man cut him off with a short bark of annoyance. "What of your sister and your other brother? What if they win?"

"That's simple," Tom said. "You and your sister will watch over them for me while I hunt for the chest. What do you say?"

"I say you are a pig."

Tom colored and balled his fists but he had the presence of mind not to do anything.

"How could you, Tom?" Sam asked.

"Go to hell."

The undergrowth cracked and snapped and Theodore Pickleman appeared. He was holding his valise and muttering to himself.

Fargo went to shout a warning but Samantha beat him to it.

"Theodore! Run! This is one of the killers!"

The lawyer stopped and looked up as if in alarm. He stared at them and then at the young assassin and then he did the last thing Fargo expected: he smiled. "I see you have matters well in hand, Jacques."

"Oui," the young man said.

"You are proving to be worth every dollar."

"What the hell?" Tom Clyborn blurted.

"You always were the slow one," Pickleman said. He walked around them and stood next to Jacques. "It is turning out better than I dared hope."

"Ou est ma soeur?"

"Eh? Your sister? Julienne is taking care of the other one." Pickleman placed the valise on the ground and beamed at Samantha and Tom. "My French is rusty but I get by."

Samantha's eyes were as wide as walnuts. "Not you."

"Yes, me," the lawyer said. "From the very beginning. I must admit it has been exhilarating."

"What do you hope to gain?"

Pickleman sighed. "Weren't any of you paying attention when I read the terms of the will? If none of you find the chest, then none of you inherit. All of your father's money and vast holdings are to be administered to benefit the poor and the needy."

"I remember that, yes. What about it?"

Pickleman rocked on his heels and chuckled in glee. "Who do you think does the administering?"

"Oh God," Sam said.

Tom was looking from her to the attorney and back again. "Oh God what? What is this all about?"

Pickleman answered him. "What it has always been about. Money. Millions and millions of dollars. Millions I will get to do with as I see fit."

Tom couldn't hide his bewilderment. "What are you talking about? If we don't get the money it's supposed to go to the poor."

"Try and follow me on this," the lawyer said with the air of an elder to a ten-year-old. "In the event that none of his children found the chest, your father appointed me executor of his estate in perpetuity. Yes, he stipulates in the will that the money is to go to the poor but *I* get to decide who exactly they are. You see, your father didn't care about that aspect. He never really expected it to come to that, I imagine."

"Wait," Tom said. "You're saying that you take over *everything*?"

"Congratulations. You're finally getting it."

"That can't be. There must be laws against it."

"Honestly, Thomas. How you manage to get dressed without help is beyond me? Certainly, there are laws. But I'm a *law*yer. I wrote up the will for your father. Every clause, every word, in such a way that after I've disposed of all of you, your father's estate and bank accounts become mine to do with as I please."

"It won't work. Someone will catch on."

"Who? The sheriff? The marshal? What cause would they have to suspect me? I assure you that the will is entirely and thoroughly legal. Not that your father read every word. He trusted me, and he could never be bothered to read a document all the way through. So I managed to slip in a few clauses he wasn't aware of." Pickleman laughed.

"But it has to go to charity," Tom persisted.

"Oh, and some of it will. To charities I set up under the table, as it were. Your mansion will become a charitable asset, and as such, mine to live in while I administer the estate." Pickleman rubbed his hands together. "Yes, sir. If I draw it out, I figure it will take a good forty to fifty years to do the administering."

"You son of a bitch."

"Now, now. Keep a civil tongue or I'll have Jacques, here, cut it out. He would, you know. He'll do anything I ask of him. Isn't that right, Jacques?"

"*Oui*, monsieur."

Fargo had listened to enough. "There are a few things I'm cloudy on yet," he admitted.

"Such as?" Pickleman said.

"Why did Jacques and his sister jump me that night on the *Yancy*?"

"Why else? I knew Sam had sent for you and I didn't want to run the risk of you finding the chest before I disposed of the heirs. I could have had them killed before this, I suppose, but the hunt was a perfect pretext. I'll say that Tom was to blame, that in his greed and his rage he murdered the others."

"Damn you," Tom snarled, and coiled to throw himself at the attorney.

"Don't," Sam said, restraining him. "You'll be dead before you take a step."

Fargo wasn't done. "Then if you hired these two, who hired Cletus Brun and Anders?"

"I hired Brun," Tom said. "How many times do I have to tell you?"

"Actually," Pickleman said, "if you'll recall, I was the one who recommended Brun to you. All the time he was working for me. I hired him and Anders, both."

"What?" Samantha and Tom said at the same time.

They weren't the only ones taken aback by the news. Jacques stiffened and said, "Did I just hear right? You hired my sister and me *and* you hired those two clods?"

"As insurance, you might say," Pickleman said. "In case you and your sister failed."

"We never fail."

"So I was told but I couldn't take the risk. I hired you and I hired them but I never told either of you about the other." Pickleman thought that was humorous. "It never occurred to me that you and your sister might catch on to them and kill them, thinking they worked for one of the Clyborns."

Sam said, "I was wrong about your assassin being a monster. You're the monster here, Theodore. You betrayed our father. You're out to destroy the rest of us. You are a vile, mean, petty little man who hid his true nature from us all these years with false smiles and false friendship."

"Oh, please. I was a whipping boy, good for running errands and attending to legal matters and nothing more."

"We've treated you like one of the family ever since I can remember."

"The family dog, perhaps." Pickleman gestured at Jacques. "Enough of this. None of them found the chest so I have no further need of them. Do as I'm paying you to do and finish them off."

"Do you have a preference as to the order?"

"Eh? No. Just kill them and be done with it."

"As you wish, monsieur."

The whole time they were talking, Fargo had slowly placed his hands flat on the ground. He dug the fingers of his right hand into the soil, uprooting a clod of dirt. It wasn't much but it was all he had and he would be damned if he was going to go down without a fight.

Jacques was taking aim at Samantha but glanced up at a sudden racket in the undergrowth.

Roland Clyborn stumbled into the open. He had been pushed from behind and was pushed again.

"Keep moving, monsieur," Julienne commanded. She saw her brother and smiled and nodded and Jacques smiled in return.

Roland fell to his knees. He had taken a fierce beating. His right eye was swollen nearly shut, his nose was broken and bleeding, his mouth dripped blood and his face was marked black-and-blue. From the way he was holding his arm, it was either sprained or broken. Pain etched his face as he looked at Theodore Pickleman and said simply, "Traitor."

The lawyer was momentarily dumbfounded. Sputtering, he croaked, "What is the meaning of this, Julienne? You were to have killed him by now while your brother attended to these others."

"*Oui*," the sister said. She had a low, melodious voice that under other circumstances would have stirred Fargo where he most liked to be stirred. "I intended to kill him, monsieur."

"What stopped you?"

Roland Clyborn managed to smile through his pulped lips. "Me. I said the magic words."

Theodore angrily shook a finger at him. "What are you prattling about? There's nothing you could say that would keep you alive."

"I found the chest."

The lawyer stiffened. "What's that?"

"You heard me, you bastard. I found the chest with the last page of Father's will."

"Where is it? I don't see it on you." Pickleman glanced at Julienne. "Do you have it?"

"*Non*, monsieur."

"Then where the hell is it?"

Julienne shrugged. "He didn't have it with him."

"Then he's lying," Pickleman practically shouted. "He tricked you into sparing him so you would bring him to me, you stupid sow."

Jacques turned and placed the muzzle of his Remington against the lawyer's head. "Have a care, monsieur. You will talk to my sister with respect or, employer or no, I will splatter your brains."

"Jacques, no," Julienne said. "He has a right to be mad if I have been made a fool of."

Jacques slowly lowered the Remington. "Very well. But he must watch his words. No man insults you while I still breathe."

Fargo had glanced at Roland and Roland at him. They understood each other without having to say anything. Fargo nodded, and Roland nodded, and Fargo tensed for what he had to do.

Pickleman was saying, "It doesn't matter if he did find the chest. So long as no one else knows we can carry on with my original plan. You'll kill them, I'll blame their deaths on Tom, and become executor of their father's estate. It's simple as can be."

"Except for one thing," Roland said.

"What would that be?"

"I took the chest to the hunting lodge and turned it over to Jarvis and the other servants for safekeeping."

"You're lying."

"You would like to think so, wouldn't you? But if you have us murdered now, you face the gallows."

"To the contrary," Pickleman said. "You've just made my alibi foolproof. I'll say that Tom went berserk when you told him you dug up the chest. He couldn't stand the thought of losing the inheritance and snapped. It's perfect."

Tom had been quiet but now he pushed to his feet and furiously declared, "You rotten scum."

"Shoot him," Pickleman said to Jacques.

The brother started to raise his revolver.

Fargo couldn't hold off any longer. He exploded up off the ground and flung the dirt in Jacques's face. Jacques instinctively ducked and sidestepped and swung the Remington toward him. Fargo sidestepped, too, as the six-gun went off. He dived, hitting Jacques low in the legs and bringing him down. He grabbed Jacques's wrist and Jacques grabbed his, and they grappled.

Pickleman was screeching for Jacques to kill him and for Julienne to help. Only Julienne couldn't.

Out of the corner of his eye Fargo glimpsed her on the ground, struggling with Roland. Despite his wounds, Roland had tackled her. He was trying to pin her and received a jolting blow to the jaw.

"Hang on!" Tom cried, and leaped to help his brother.

Fargo winced as a knee caught him high on his leg. It had missed his groin by inches. He returned the favor and Jacques grunted but his grip didn't weaken.

Hissing, the young assassin bared his teeth. "I have wanted a rematch with you."

Jacques drove his forehead against Fargo's chin.

The world burst into fragments of swirling colors. Fargo lost his hold. A blow to his chest knocked him onto his side.

His vision cleared, and he saw Jacques already rising and the revolver being pointed at him. He was about to die and there was nothing he could do.

That was when Theodore Pickleman darted in and grabbed Jacques by the arm. "Kill them!" he shrieked. "You must kill them, do you hear?"

"Let go, you fool!" Jacques threw him off .

By then Fargo was up. He seized Jacques by the wrist just as the revolver went off and the lead dug a furrow in the earth. Pivoting, Fargo heaved and threw his foot out. Jacques's legs and head switched places and Jacques's arm gave a terrific wrench and a *snap*.

Jacques screamed.

"Brother!" Julienne cried.

Fargo glimpsed her battling Roland and Tom. She had lost her pistol and had a knife in each hand. It was two against one but Fargo knew they were no match for her. He had to help, only he wasn't give the chance.

Jacques came up off the ground with a knife of his own. He stabbed at Fargo's chest and Fargo twisted aside. Jacques came after him, cutting, slashing, trying to bring Fargo down.

Samantha called out Tom's name in horror.

Fargo glanced over. Tom was down, crimson misting from a wound in his side. Now only Roland prevented the sister from coming to the aid of her brother, and Roland wouldn't last long alone.

A grim grin curled Jacques's mouth. His next several swings were intended to keep Fargo at bay until Julienne could spring to his side.

Jacques had dropped the Remington when Fargo broke his arm, and apparently forgotten about it. Fargo hadn't. There it was, almost at his feet. He kicked at Jacques, forcing Jacques back, and dropped to his knee.

"Non!"

Jacques had seen the revolver.

Fargo scooped it up. The grips molded to his palm and he thumbed back the hammer.

Jacques raised the knife to slash.

Fargo fired as Jacques leaped at him, fired as Jacques twisted to the impact, fired as Jacques sought to sink the knife in his neck, fired as Jacques swayed and fired as Jacques tottered and fired the last cartridge in the cylinder into Jacques's forehead.

"Noooooo!"

The wail was torn from Julienne. Roland was down, and she started toward Fargo, blood dripping from both her knives.

Fargo whirled, the Remington held low. He figured she hadn't counted the shots because she spun and bolted into the trees. He didn't hesitate. He went after her.

Samantha shouted his name but Fargo didn't slow. Julienne wasn't the kind to forgive and forget. If he didn't catch her here and now, if he didn't end it, she would come after him later and exact her vengeance at a time and place of her choosing.

But God, she was fast. Fargo had been in a footrace once against some of the fastest runners in the country, including an Apache girl famed for her speed, and Julienne was every whit their equal. He kept her in sight but it took all he had. She flew through the vegetation as if she had wings on her feet. She looked back once and only once, and did a strange thing; she smiled.

Fargo concentrated on running and nothing but running. He avoided a pine and vaulted a stump and lost a few yards.

Up ahead were a cluster of big oaks. Julienne streaked in among them—and disappeared.

Fargo reached the oaks and stopped. There wasn't much undergrowth. He figured she had ducked behind a trunk and was waiting to ambush him. Warily, he advanced, holding the Remington by the barrel. He passed several trees without seeing sign of her.

155

A sound overhead caused Fargo to glance up. Julienne had just launched herself from a tree limb. He dodged but wasn't quite quick enough and felt a stinging sensation in his right shoulder. She had cut him. He whirled toward her as she alighted in a crouch. He swung the revolver like a club.

With incredible swiftness, Julienne dodged. Before Fargo could draw his arm back, a knife flashed and blood welled. She had cut him again. He retreated a few steps and she came after him.

"For what you did to Jacques I will kill you piece by piece. You will be a long time dying."

"Big talk, bitch," Fargo said to goad her. He watched her knives, only her knives. When the left blade swept at him he was ready and skipped aside. The other knife flicked at his neck but he slipped out of reach.

"You are uncommonly quick, monsieur."

"Your brother said the same thing shortly before I blew him to hell."

Julienne's features hardened. Her eyes were smoldering volcanoes. She came in fast and she came in low, windmilling both blades, a human threshing machine bent on his destruction.

Fargo backpedaled. He ducked. He weaved and turned, always a hairsbreadth from harm. But he couldn't keep it up. Sooner or later she would bring him down.

The tip of a knife narrowly missed Fargo's throat. The keen edge of the other caught his wrist.

Fargo drew back as if in pain and again she came after him. He wanted her to. He cocked his arm as if to club her with the revolver and when she jerked back he threw it with all his strength and hit her full in the face. She cried out and blood sprayed; then Fargo had her by the wrists and she was twisting and pulling to break free and he was trying to hurl her to the ground.

Fargo had seldom encountered a woman so strong. He locked a foot behind her leg and sought to trip her. With amazing agility Julienne hopped over his leg and her right foot rose and caught him on the side of the head. His ear flared with agony. She hopped again and this time kicked him in the side of the neck.

A part of Fargo admired her skill. She was one of the toughest fighters he had ever tangled with. He tried to pin her arms but she was as slippery as a wet eel. She kicked him in the leg, in the ribs.

Fargo was losing. He was bleeding and tired and growing weak. But she wasn't the only one who could kick. He buried his boot in her gut and she doubled over. With a wrench, he tore the knife from her right hand, reversed his grip, and as she straightened, sank the blade to the hilt in her eye.

Julienne arched her back and her mouth parted. Incredulity widened her other eye; then she oozed to the ground and lay quaking before she subsided and was still.

"Damn," Fargo said.

Tom Clyborn had been stabbed in the lungs. He lingered two days in a bed at the hunting lodge attended by a doctor from Hannibal. His last words, Samantha told Fargo, were a question. "All I ever wanted in life was to be rich. Was that too much to ask?" He had laughed bitterly, and died.

Roland's arm was in a sling. Broken in two places, the doctor said. He was battered and bandaged and would be a long while healing but he would live.

The sheriff took Theodore Pickleman into custody. The lawyer had tried to run off after Fargo shot Jacques but Sam snatched up a rock and beaned him with it.

As for the chest that cost so many their lives, Fargo went to the creek the next day with a shovel and Samantha and began poking around the willow trees that lined the near bank.

"Why the willows?"

"Don't you remember what Pickleman told us your father said to him?" Fargo reminded her. It had stuck in his craw and he finally figured out why.

"Something about whoever found the chest wouldn't have any cause to weep—" Sam stopped. "A weeping willow! Why didn't I think of that?"

"I could be wrong."

He wasn't. The earth near the sixth willow they came to had recently been disturbed. Fargo dug down a few inches and there it was: a small wooden chest with a folded sheet of paper inside. He let Sam take the paper out. She unfolded it, and frowned.

"I thought you'd be happy."

"This cost me three brothers and a sister." Sam's eyes filled with tears. "I'll have the last laugh on Father, though. I'm sharing everything equally with Roland."

"Good for you."

Sam shook herself. Grinning, she put her hand on his. "There's something I'd like to share with you if you don't mind coming up to my bedroom. Are you interested, kind sir?"

"What do you think?" Fargo laughed and smacked her on the fanny.

LOOKING FORWARD!
The following is the opening
section of the next novel in the exciting
***Trailsman* series from Signet:**

THE TRAILSMAN #341
SIERRA SIX-GUNS

California, 1859—A storm is coming to Kill Creek.

Skye Fargo liked the Sierra Nevada Mountains. They were
miles high. They were remote. Lush forest covered the lower
slopes, snow capped the high peaks.

Unlike back East, where much of the wildlife had been
killed off to fill supper pots, animal life was everywhere.
Ponderous grizzlies were on perpetual prowl, tawny mountain lions glided through shadowed woodlands, hungry wolves
roved in packs. Elk, deer, mountain sheep, and a host of smaller
creatures were the prey the predators fed on.

On a sunny autumn morning, Fargo drew rein on a switch-
back on a mountain no white man had ever set foot on and
breathed deep of the crisp air.

A big man, he wore buckskins and a white hat brown with
dust. A red bandanna around his neck had seen a lot of use.
So had the Colt on his hip and the Arkansas toothpick snug

in an ankle sheath. His eyes were as blue as a small lake below. His beard was neatly trimmed.

Fargo gigged the Ovaro. He was on his way to San Francisco and had decided to spend a week or so alone in the high country. He liked to do that every now and then. It reminded him of why he enjoyed the wild places so much.

Fargo loved to roam where no one had gone before. Where most men kept their gaze on the ground and the next step they were about to take, his gaze was always on the far horizon. He had to see what lay over it.

A game trail made the descent easy. A lot of creatures came to the lake daily to slake their thirst.

Fargo was almost to the bottom when he spied two does. They jerked their heads up but they weren't looking at him. They stared intently at a thicket that bordered the shore. Suddenly wheeling, they bounded off, their tails erect.

Fargo wondered what had spooked them. It could be just about anything. Deer were easily frightened. Still, to be safe, he reined up and watched the thicket. A minute went by and nothing appeared so he clucked to the Ovaro and rode to the water's edge. Dismounting, he let the reins dangle, and he stretched. He had been in the saddle since sunup.

Sinking to one knee, Fargo dipped a hand in the lake. The water was cold and clear. He sipped and smacked his lips. "How about you, big fella?"

As if the stallion understood, it lowered its muzzle.

"Not too much now." Fargo had a habit of talking to the stallion as if it were a person. Often, it was his only companion for days at a time.

The stallion went on drinking.

High in the sky a bald eagle soared. In the forest a squirrel scampered from limb to limb. Out on the lake a fish broke the surface. The day was peaceful and perfect, exactly as Fargo liked them.

Then the Ovaro raised its head and pricked its ears and nickered.

Fargo looked, and froze.

A dog had come out of the thicket. A huge dog, almost four feet high at the front shoulders and bulky enough to weigh upwards of two hundred pounds. It had a blunt face with a broad jaw and a thick barrel of a body. Its color was somewhere between brown and gray. At the moment it was standing still, its dark eyes fixed intently on him.

"Hell," Fargo said. Where there was a dog there were bound to be people and he had hoped to fight shy of them for a spell.

The dog took a step and growled.

Fargo smiled and gestured. "I'm friendly, boy. You'd be wise to be the same." Out of habit he placed his hand on his Colt. He wasn't worried. If the dog came at him he could drop it before it covered half the distance.

From behind him came the crack of a twig.

Fargo glanced over his shoulder.

Another dog, the same breed and about the same size, had emerged from the woods. Its hackles were raised and its lips were drawn back. Its teeth looked to be wickedly sharp.

"Damn." Fargo didn't like this. He stepped to the Ovaro and snagged the reins and was about to slip his boot into the stirrups when a sound caused him to whirl.

A third dog wasn't more than ten feet away. Its huge head held low, it crouched.

"Down boy." Fargo scanned the shore for sign of the owner but saw no one. He quickly mounted. He figured to get out of there before the dogs decided to attack.

The nearest dog moved to a point between the stallion and the woods, blocking his way.

"Son of a bitch." Fargo was trying to recollect where he had seen dogs like these before. Then it came to him—Saint

Louis, some time back. Mastiffs, they were called. He seemed to recall they were bred in England or some such place, but he could be mistaken.

The dog to the right and the dog to the left moved slowly toward him.

"Go away, damn you." It occurred to Fargo that if they rushed him he might drop one or two but not all three, and all it would take was one to bring the Ovaro down. He didn't dare risk that. Suddenly reining toward the lake, he used his spurs.

The stallion reacted superbly, as it nearly always did. It took a long bound and plunged into the water.

Fargo bent forward and hiked his boots out of the stirrups. The Ovaro would swim to the other side and he would be on his way, no worse for the bother. He chuckled, pleased at how he had outwitted the dogs, confident they wouldn't come after him. He shifted in the saddle to be sure.

All three mastiffs jumped in. The nearest surged swiftly after the Ovaro, swimming with powerful strokes, its head high, its teeth glistening in the sunlight.

"Damn dumb dogs." Fargo was growing mad. He'd tried to spare them, and now look. He drew his Colt and took aim but changed his mind and holstered it. So far the Ovaro was holding its own. If he could stay ahead of them until he reached the other side, he could get away. The dogs might be fast but over a long distance the Ovaro's stamina would win out.

The bottom of Fargo's pants were soaked. He would have to dry them and his boots and socks later. But at least his saddlebags and bedroll were mostly dry. The Henry in the saddle scabbard was getting wet and he would have to dry and clean it later, a chore he could do without.

Fargo checked behind him. The nearest dog hadn't gained

any and the others had no chance in hell of catching him before he struck solid ground.

Several ducks took noisy wing, frightened by the commotion.

The dogs didn't give up.

Fargo wished he knew who their owner was. He'd pistol-whip the bastard for letting them run free. It made him wonder what anyone was doing there, so far from anywhere.

The Ovaro swam smoothly, tirelessly.

Fargo's gaze drifted to the shore they were making for and a tingle of alarm rippled down his spine. "It can't be."

A fourth dog had emerged from the forest and was pacing back and forth, waiting for them.

"What is this, the whole litter?" Fargo grumbled. He reined the stallion to the right. The mastiff on the shore moved in the same direction. Fargo reined to the left. The dog moved to cut him off. Once again Fargo drew the Colt. He had nothing against dogs but he would be damned if he'd let them attack him. As soon as he was close enough, the beast on shore was dead.

They were awfully well trained, Fargo reflected, and was struck by a hunch. He scoured the vegetation and was about convinced his hunch must be wrong when a shadow detached itself from a tree. He couldn't see clearly enough to tell if the figure was white or red but since Indians seldom had mastiffs he took it for granted it was a white man and hollered, "Call your damn dogs off!"

The shadow didn't respond.

"Did you hear me?" Fargo raised the Colt. "Call them off or you'll bury them."

The figure stepped into the open.

Fargo half wanted to pinch himself. "Lord almighty," he blurted in amazement.

It was a woman. She couldn't be much over twenty. Luxurious red hair cascaded over her slender shoulders, framing an oval face as lovely as any female's ever born. Her clothes consisted of a homespun shirt and britches that might have been painted on. She had an hourglass shape and a full bosom, and was barefoot. One hand was on her shapely hip and in the other she held a six-gun, which she now trained on Fargo. "You shoot any of my dogs, mister, and I'll sure as blazes shoot you."

Fargo's mouth moved of its own accord. "Then call them off, you idiot."

The girl's face became as red as her hair. "You best keep away, you hear? We don't cotton to strangers. It's ours and ours alone."

"What is?"

"I've said all I'm going to." The redhead put two fingers to her mouth and let out with a piercing whistle. Immediately, the dog on the shore turned and trotted toward her.

Fargo looked back. The dogs in the lake were veering toward her, as well. He turned toward the forest again—and she was nowhere to be seen. "What the hell?"

Fargo was tempted to go after her but he had the Ovaro to think of. He continued on, and presently the stallion had solid ground under its hooves and was out of the lake and dripping wet.

The three dogs bolted into the woods as soon as they were out of the water.

"So much for them," Fargo said in mild disgust for the inconvenience they had caused. He resumed his interrupted journey. When he reached the far end of the lake he stopped and glanced back, seeking some sign of the girl and her pack. He wondered who she was. A homesteader, he reckoned, which meant a cabin must be nearby. It bothered him. He never expected to find another living soul this deep in the mountains.

With a shrug, Fargo clucked to the stallion. He had never been in this particular part of the Sierra Nevadas before and he was eager to explore. A fir-covered slope brought him to a ridge. He stopped to look down at the lake and blinked in surprise.

The girl and her dogs were staring up at him.

Fargo smiled and waved. It might do to show her he could be as friendly as the next gent.

The girl pointed up at him and said something to the dogs and all four bounded up the slope.

Fargo couldn't believe this was happening. It looked as if she had sent her pets after him. Cupping a hand to his mouth, he shouted, "What the hell are you doing? Call them back! Now!"

The girl just stood and stared.

Swearing lustily, Fargo hauled on the reins and used his spurs. He went down the far side of the ridge and came to a narrow valley. Bursting from the woods, he stuck to open ground and brought the stallion to a gallop. There was no way in hell the mastiffs could catch him now.

Half a mile of hard riding brought Fargo to a bend. He thundered around it and abruptly drew rein, dumbfounded by the unexpected sight that unfolded before him.

To the north reared broken bluffs, a creek meandering along their base.

To the south along the flank of the valley were over a score of buildings, most made from planks and a few from logs and the rest slapped together using whatever was handy. A single street dotted by several hitch rails and a water trough ran the length of the town.

"I'll be damned." Fargo had no inkling he was anywhere

near civilization. So far as he knew, there shouldn't be a town or settlement within a hundred miles.

Hell, make that two hundred. He tapped his spurs and rode closer and the truth dawned.

The street was thick with dust. One of the hitch rails was broken and the water trough was dry. The wear and tear of neglect showed on every building; roofs sagged, windows were broken, overhang posts had tilted or were cracked. Moved by the breeze, a single batwing on a saloon creaked noisily.

It was a *ghost* town.

Fargo rode to the near end of the street and drew rein. A small sign, faded but readable, told him the town's name. "Kill Creek," he said out loud. He rose in the stirrups and surveyed the creek and spotted a long-abandoned dredge. The dredge explained everything.

Back in 'forty-nine, gold was found at Sutter's Mill. A horde of people from all over the country and from all walks of life flocked to the California mountains hoping to strike it rich. That so few ever did didn't deter them. Each thought they would be the one. Thousands more came to provide food and lodging and whatever else the gold seekers needed.

Towns sprang up virtually overnight. All it took was for someone to find a nugget or two, or pan a poke's worth. Word would spread like a prairie fire.

Almost always, the new strikes were short-lived, and once there was no more gold to be had, the horde moved on to the next strike. In their wake they left abandoned towns and deserted camps.

Kill Creek was one of those towns.

That Fargo had never heard of it didn't surprise him. There were dozens just like it, forgotten and empty of everything save bugs and dust.

He rode down the street until he came to the creaking batwing. It wouldn't hurt to rest a spell. He was about to climb down when something squeaked and a rat came scuttling from between two of the buildings, ran out into the middle of the street, promptly wheeled, and ran back into the shadows again.

"It's my day for stupid animals," Fargo said, and chuckled. It died in his throat the very next moment.

Around the bend at the other end of town loped the four huge mastiffs.

Running shoulder to shoulder, their sleek muscles rippling under their hides, they made straight for Kill Creek.

And for him.

No other series packs this much heat!

THE TRAILSMAN

**Follow the trail of the gun-slinging heroes of
Penguin's Action Westerns at
penguin.com/actionwesterns**